NO TURNING BACK

EROTIC VAMPIRE PARANORMAL

SHALA BREECE

plicit Press

CHAPTER 1

VAMPIRES HAVE A WAY WITH WOMEN. It's in their eyes and their touch. They're not as cold as they've often been made out to be; at least not the younger, newer ones. Their body temperature lowers slowly, but over hundreds of years. So you don't know you're sleeping with one until it's too late. Human beings just don't have the facility for being fucked so hard. They enjoy it; completely...they just don't survive it.

So the vampires don't use their attractiveness to woo long-term lovers. They just use it to lull unsuspecting females into their beds. This is something that they do with malice almost, knowing that mortals couldn't possibly survive the connection, but needing to test it anyway. Tonight the vampires are feeling amorous again. And their target is the village convent. Who could resist so many virgins in one place?

The nuns are asleep. They're mainly women in their early twenties who had heard from legend that crosses warded off the evil that had been plaguing the Italian countryside for a while now. But they'd also heard of many cases where women have been found dead, the telltale puncture wounds on their breasts or necks, even though they had a rosary on their person. So these virgins thought that they would be safest at the convent, where crosses are aplenty, and just for good measure, god lives there too.

But they thought wrong. And now as they sleep, another night wrapped up in a false sense of security, the halls of the convent are being patrolled by an army of vampires with a need to feed, and hard cocks. The vampires are practically salivating at the smell of untouched cunt and pure blood. There will be no need for a scene here, the convent lending itself to a quiet dinner...

Vampires have an interesting frequency that matches the pheromones secreted by women when they are aroused. They call it their sleeper vibration, not so much because it puts women to sleep, but because it makes them easier to sleep with. It also confuses the circuitry of the human brain and makes the women in range believe that they are in a dream. This is one of the reasons vampires can kill without being detected; and why vampire victims are mostly women. There are seldom any screams.

These vibrations permeate through the convent quickly. It's that time of the night many of the women in the sacred space are already half asleep anyway, and as such, their pussies are going through their natural processes, releasing what the vampires need for their dealings here to be silent. Soon the vampires are no longer gliding along, in midair, to avoid being heard. They walk boldly on the ancient stone floors, knowing that the available cunts are just about good and ready.

The virginities start to fall in minutes. Credo is a

viscous nightwalker with a passion for fucking. He lets the others settle into their chosen pussy and he continues down the dark passageways, sensing that an even more delicious treat awaits him at the end of the cavern. He reaches the door to the chapel and nudges it open.

To his delight, there are three ethereal-looking, dark-haired women who had decided to come to midnight prayers just before the vampires arrived. The women are on the floor, a confused look on their faces. Credo knows already that this is going to be fun, especially since these three still have a little awareness in them. He can't wait for the look on their faces when they realize that this is not a dream.

"Ladies..." He lets the sound of his voice linger and lands in waves on each of them. He watches as they try to mouth the questions in their heads...

"Shhh...no need for theatrics...I'm going to make it as pleasant for you as possible..." Again he is almost rolling the words from his mouth and into the space around the three virgin's heads.

He is on the first woman, choosing the one in the middle so that the others can watch, building their arousal, and their fear. They can't move, not sure which way is up. Credo has been a vampire for a long time. He knows just how to lull his victims with his vibrations. He also knows how to literally stun them using nothing but the erotic depth of his tone. It is this semi-shock that renders them motionless for the most part.

He pulls them a little closer together so that he can touch all three of them at the same time. He knows it won't be long before the chapel fills with other vampires, the smell of the three women's pussies heavy in the air. This will be irresistible to the others too, who will probably leave whoever they're fucking to come and sip from this stream. Credo is a master and maximizes feminine arousal. The cunt he is working with always smells the best.

Credo takes all his clothes off, liking the feeling of his nakedness. He has a large, strong body, and a thick, long cock with a massive head. Just the sight of him sends anxious chills into any woman who is about to be joined to him. He gets the other nightdresses off too and smells each of their pussies in turn before licking them gently. Convent or not, a pussy will respond as a pussy should, despite the owner's resistance, provided you approached it well. Credo always approaches it well, loving wet, slimy cunt. And he has yet to encounter a pussy that offers up any resistance to his beauty.

After tasting all three cunts with his mouth, his tongue going in to ensure that the vaginal walls are dripping in pussy juice, he focuses a little more intently on the vagina in the middle. All three have their eyes glassy from arousal but as large as small plates from fear. These three know that they can't possibly be inhabiting the same dream. They know this is real.

Then Credo sends his cock into the woman under him, filling her to the point of overwhelming her pussy and her head. She all but gags. He shoots straight through her virginity and immediately starts fucking her as though he were fucking an experienced whore, happy that he has primed her pussy and that she is wet enough to receive him completely. Her cunt is so delicious that Credo already regrets that he probably won't be able to settle inside it for too long.

Each stroke, each incredible thrust rips straight through the vaginal passage, wrapping the nun in so much ecstasy that she is unable to look at him, grateful that the sounds of her pleasure are only in her head. She can't have the others know that she is in absolute heaven. Credo already has his fingers in the pussies on either side of him, preparing them for the cock that is already proving too much for the woman he is fucking.

The exaggerated smell of female fear and cunt is heavy in the air now. Credo is on to his second charge, the first not making it long enough for him to have an orgasm. This always happens with him. So he very rarely tries to have sex if he isn't assured of at least three punanies. He can usually get off with three. His cock is as cold and hard as steel. It pierces through the pussy like a blade, cutting pleasure into every part of the woman being fed this steel. He hates that these women with their warm blood and hot cunts are so weak.

He senses movement in the hallway outside and starts to thrust even harder. He will not be happy if he doesn't have an orgasm, at least one. He fucks harder and harder and then stops, sensing that even this woman hasn't managed to hold on, despite her own attempts to reach the orgasm she had no idea she wanted to have. Credo has literally crucified her with his cock. Cursing loudly he pulls his dick from her and picks up the third. He goes into the door at the far end of the chapel, into a smaller room, and pushes the furniture against the door. He lays her on the couch so that he can hold the door closed with his own strength while he fucks her.

Credo slides his cock into her warmth fast, stroking her face as the erotic screams in her head show up only in her eyes. Her entire body is stiff as it fights this invasion. Her cunt isn't putting up the same fight, every part of her vagina slippery and wet thanks to the prolonged fingering she received. Credo gets deep inside her. He goes too deep too often and it's clear that he is losing her too.

He closes his eyes, pushes hard against the door that is being banged on already, the others wanting in on the action, and thrusts until his cock shoots his finally immortal seed into the woman who has just lost her own race toward the climax. He pulls his dick from her and lets the door slide open. The room fills with his friends and he goes off to find his clothes and perhaps another trio of cunts that he can empty his dick into...

Just down the hill, halfway between the convent and the village, Arianna wakes from yet another nightmare. Even after hundreds of years, her memories haunt her. In the damp darkness of the farmer's shed, which is her home for the night, she wonders if she will be able to feed tonight. She had heard the farmer's wife earlier in the evening discussing with a neighbor how the mayor was beating up his wife. This wife-beater would make for a delicious meal. Men who hurt women are her favorite food. She fuels her rage by deliberately remembering the men who took her life as she knew it from her centuries ago and left her like this; an animal that needs warm blood to live. But the vessels she feeds from don't deserve to live. It is this thought that makes it easy for Arianna to feed.

She catches a scent in the air that has nothing to do with the animals that lived in the shed before the dark death that saw most of the livestock in the village destroyed. Her instincts start to fire and she leaves the safety of the wooden structure. The night air is crisp. It feels like midnight. She looks toward the village, breathing in the direction of the breeze. Then she looks up the hill at the convent with its hazy candles burning in some of the windows. Again she breathes in the scent riding in on the wind. Arianna knows this smell.

It takes her less than a minute to fly up to where the fusion of cunt, cock, and vampire-induced fear is heaviest in the air. She can smell the vampires like old meat on a lazy butcher's porch. She knows some of them from previous battles. As she enters the convent she tries in vain to get a sense of human life. There is nothing. Faint heartbeats register momentarily, flutter, and fade. She is too late.

Arianna listens to the men, monsters like her, gloat about the work they've just done. She can smell the women still on their cocks. She can smell the life ended on the tips of their fangs. She hates them. It was a gang like this that changed her. It was a gang like this that left her for dead without making sure. It was a rogue gang like this that turned her into this powerful, undead thing, powerful enough to make sure that the undead who did terrible things like this, actually died.

She knows she is outnumbered. But she must avenge the women now spread throughout the convent in strange contortions, their legs wide open, dripping with vampire semen that smells like death, decorated like trophies for the final amusement of these vipers. So Arianna gathers her hate into the palms of her hands and tears through the convent, intent on ripping the vampires' heads from their shoulders one at a time.

She is quick, grabbing two at once and pulling them closer to her than she likes them to be.

"Vipers..." Arianna hisses the words.

"Fuck you, Arianna..." The vampire hiss right back.

They know who she is. And they know that she is strong. Arianna is a formidable opponent because she has the balls to feed on men. Testosterone powers her up, like the secret potions of the ancients. Vampire men rely on their inherent strength and so they are comfortable drinking the blood of women. Women are also easier. And they have pussies. It is this arrogance on the part of the vampires that really pisses Arianna off. There is no stopping her as one by one she kills off these bastards that have turned what should have been a quiet night, into a nightmare.

Arianna rips off their heads and watches as they disintegrate. Then she moves on to find the others. The sound of her name fills the convent. Many of them try to flee, knowing what she is capable of. Some come to her, believing that they can bring her down. Of course, they don't. They can't. Arianna goes through them like a wolf among lambs. It isn't long before she has done all the damage needed for the majority of the vampires to be dead.

There is silence now in the convent. The hissing has stopped. She has done her job. She knows that the incompleteness that comes over her means that she hasn't managed to get all of them. She focuses on the traces of the vibrations still hanging in the air. They fade slowly. But two linger. Two of the vampires have managed to escape. She hates these cowards who can't face her, instead of running off to the Leadership to report that vigilante Arianna is at it again. But at least she knows that they are afraid of her. And as long as they fear her, as long as she is a nuisance to the Leadership, an elite body of elder vampires who run the World Order of Vampires, she knows that she is doing something right.

But now she has to run, again. The Leadership will be sending an army for her, vicious bounty hunters desperate for the treasure they've been promised for her head. They don't want her alive. She's been told this by many a hunter just before she's removed their heads instead. So Arianna heads for the beach, the only place she can really think of. And the only place where her senses are peaked and she is most difficult to surprise.

If only she knew where The Leadership based itself, where their headquarters were. But vampires so powerful would never risk staying in one place too long. There are many disloyal to them who would like to see them replaced. Arianna knows this. And the only real collateral that The Leadership has is that they are the custodians of the scrolls that serve as a register for every vampire on earth, and also a clear manual on how each of these vampires can be killed. Every clan has a weakness. And every weakness can be exploited.

The beach is quiet. But it is also cold. Arianna hates the cold, something that has stayed with her from her mortal childhood. She holds on to this hate because it is the only thing that reminds her that she was once human. There are lovers somewhere further along down the beach, snug in a cove. She imagines a small fire, a blanket. She can smell what they are doing under the blanket. She is sad that she will never know that kind of loving. Real and human, with the urgency that comes from knowing that you don't have forever that makes it valuable.

She finds her own cove and tries to sense for anything that should not be here. When nothing irritates her senses she huddles on the ground and tries to sleep. She won't feed tonight. One night won't kill her. And the mayor will still be a wife-beating asshole tomorrow. Her eyes close easily thanks to the exhaustion from the fight. But her dreams are again not as easy as the sleep that carries her to them. She's soon back in her dream as though it was yesterday...

It was almost eight hundred years earlier when she was turned. Arianna was a beautiful, young woman who promised to marry a man she actually loved. She had held on to her virtue from the day she met Sven, knowing that her body, like her heart, would one day be his alone. But then they came. And nothing was ever the same again; not for Arianna; not for anybody.

The day was soaked in the spring sun and Arianna, twenty-three and perfect, piercing eyes and raven locks, was browning her skin in the meadow. Her wedding and so her wedding night was to be the next day. She wanted to be perfect for her husband. But as usual, and much to her parent's dismay, she fell asleep. When she woke up it was already evening and the sun had gone to its resting place for the next day.

The stars lit the sky so brightly that she could see clear across the field and make out the houses on their farm. She walked quickly through the long grass, not wanting her brothers to be sent out to look for her because they were always upset if she interrupted their rest after a long day in the fields. But she didn't make it very far.

"What's the hurry miss?" The words seemed to come from all around her and inside her head all at once.

Arianna looks around, knowing that these five men that suddenly surround her cannot be human. They looked like humans, very beautiful humans, and they spoke like humans. But where did they come from, and how was it that they weren't running next to her? They just seemed to glide through the air alongside her as she held her skirt high and kept her focus on the lights almost in reach, the safety that she knew she would find with her father.

But she doesn't make it. The vampires let her run until she is too tired to scream but close enough to home to be heard if she did. They drop her to the ground and position her so that she can practically see into the kitchen as her mother finishes up with dinner. She can see her brothers reluctantly putting on their coats to go out and look for her in the meadow. She hears her dogs barking.

"Father... father..." Arianna knows that the words are barely a whisper as they leave her mouth.

Then a haze comes over her along with a chill as her clothing comes off. The chill doesn't last long as mouths and tongues start to work between her legs and on her breasts. Arianna closes her eyes, unsure suddenly if this was a dream. It feels like a dream.

"Mama..." Arianna calls for her mother. The sound doesn't come. The words are there but the sounds simply will not come. She screams for her brothers, her father, and her dogs. No sound comes from her mouth and so nobody comes to help her. Her thoughts go to Sven as fingers start to pry open her cunt and she knows that he would not be her first. She knows that he would never be her anything.

She remembers the smell of death. She had smelled death in the meadow before, and in the barn when a heifer refused to give up a stillborn calf. This smell was thick in the air. But this heinous smell seemed to be secondary now as her body started to tingle, her pussy pulsating, her clit beating the same rhythm between her legs as it was in her head. Arianna had never touched a cock, or seen one that wasn't her brothers' until that night when five vampires filled her with their pipes. She knew that that isn't how it was meant to be. She knew it wouldn't have been that way with Sven.

The sound of their voices too lingered in the air along with their smell. They joked as they took turns trying to see whose cock would deal the death blow. Her pussy filled with a cold slime that reminded her of the moss on the rocks by the river. She hated it. She wanted death to come because she hated that she was enjoying every part of it, at least her body was, and there was nothing she could do about it. Arianna knew that her life would never be the same after this violation. The last thing she remembers is a stabbing pain in her neck, the last vampire fucking her biting into her as he emptied more of his slime into her. When she woke naked in the field, she knew that she was no longer Arianna...

For the second time, tonight Arianna is ripped from her sleep by this haunting dream. If only it was just a dream. But it is a memory etched deep inside her skull. And no matter how many women she saves, it just won't go away. She will have to deal with it for the rest of her long life, distracted momentarily by the changes she sees in the world.

The lovers are still at it in the cove somewhere down the beach. And since it's clear that Arianna won't be getting any sleep tonight either, she moves silently toward the sounds of lovemaking. She likes to watch humans making love when there is emotion and desire involved. It makes her feel things that she normally wouldn't allow herself to feel.

She was right about the blanket. But the couple isn't underneath it. They are locked together tight on top of it. Arianna finds a perch where she can watch them without the embers from their fire catching her shadow. The last thing she wants is to interrupt this beautifully intimate moment.

The man is strong. She can tell this from the way his muscles move as he works over his maiden. She is on her back, her legs spread far, willing him to feed her every part of himself. She grabs his head and her own each time he thrusts into her. Both of them make the most magnificent sounds; sounds that they can only make here on a deserted beach in the early darkness of the morning.

Arianna watches as this Italian moves like water over

the woman he loves. He feeds her all his strength, filling her pussy with his dick. She wishes she could see how much dick it is but she can't. What she can see are his massive balls between his parted legs each time he moves. It's a beautiful sight.

The woman wraps her arms around him and he rolls over so that she is on top. Again the movement is fluid. The light catches her breasts perfectly, even the sweat running down them glistens. Arianna allows herself to tingle inside her own cunt. She would give anything for this man to be Sven and for her to be the woman riding his cock so intensely that her breasts dance in the dark.

She moves around and around on her lover and Arianna watches the man's face. He is completely satisfied with this woman. He is honored that she is his. This is what love is. This is what lovemaking is. This is what Arianna will never know. She looks away, hurting. Her hate comes up inside her again like acid and she wants to kill something. She will have another opportunity to rip the heads off the vampires who changed her. She knows she will. So she goes back to watching the show, a welcome distraction from the version in her head.

The man takes hold of the woman by her waist and turns her around on his dick so that she is now facing away from him. He gives a few more strokes before taking hold of her breasts and easing her down on him. Then he rolls them onto their sides and continues driving his cock into her like the waves of the ocean. She lifts her leg and he takes it in his hand. As he thrusts out Arianna gets a look at the thick rod that this woman is allowing into herself so easily. Human beings are clearly designed to make love with each other. This woman loves this massive rod inside her. She doesn't deny an inch of it the pleasures that she holds inside herself.

The tingle moves from Arianna's cunt up through her belly and into her breasts. Then she feels it on the entire surface of her skin. She wants this intimacy. She craves it. But it just isn't possible. She is a predator. Who could possibly do such a beautiful thing with an animal like her, regardless of how she looks.

Suddenly Arianna is distracted from somewhere inside. Her instincts are going crazy and the tingle is starting to fade, replaced rapidly by anxiety and then an acute awareness of danger. Only she knows that it is danger, the fusion of pheromones and the vampires' vibrations letting her know that the bastards are at it again. She leaves the cove quietly while the lovers continue loving each other.

Arianna goes high up over the rocks to get an idea of where the danger is. The sea spray comes at her, the smell of wet fanny fused with salt. She knows that a woman is in trouble. The woman probably doesn't even know yet that she is in danger. This is the burden of youth, naivety. Arianna must find her before it is too late.

She comes around a flat rock jutting out of the sand that seems to reach toward the sky. A woman in her early twenties is caught between two vampires. They have her on the sand, one parting her legs, the other one with his fingers, then his tongue in her mouth. The woman is in a blissful state, fingers now moving in and out of her pussy as it becomes increasingly wet. These vampires are clearly the kind that likes to play with their food.

"You're going to be tasty..." The one with his fingers in the woman takes the finger from her cunt and places it in his mouth. She smiles, losing herself to the pleasure being sent through her, oblivious to the many warnings she received from her friends when she decided on a beach walk with the two handsome strangers. Another finger goes back into her.

"That looks like fun..." Arianna speaks in a whisper so low that she knows only the vampires will hear. They look up, spotting her mid-air just above them.

"Arianna..." They know who she is. They've heard that she is in the area. They will not allow her to interrupt their fun or their feed. The vampires give off another shot of their vibration just to ensure their catch doesn't escape while they take care of Arianna. The woman falls to the ground, half asleep, half not.

The vampires battle just above the sand. Arianna is on top form tonight and a head drops, followed shortly by a body that it is no longer attached to. There is an amber glow, then a gray just before the corpse becomes ash and blows along the coast with the sand. The second vampire is a little bit more of a challenge. He keeps Arianna in the air for a while and then pins her on the ground. He takes firm hold of her head and starts to pull and twist.

She reaches for his erection and sends her nails into the flesh of his cock. He tries to free himself without losing his hold on her head. She digs in deeper and tears at the flesh. He is suddenly off her, inspecting the damage. His arrogance is his downfall. As he watches the blood fall from his dick Arianna shoots up and then behind him.

She grabs his hair and pulls his head back hard, reaching around and gripping his dick at the same time. She pulls hard on his stiffness and rips his cock from his groin. He screams and she shoves it into his mouth. Then she shoots up higher and swings her body around violently in the air. There is a snap as body and then head falls onto the sand, glow for a second, and are gone.

Arianna goes to where the woman is, still in her dream

state. She is lucid but not awake, sort of aware now of what she has just witnessed. Arianna takes her into the water and both of them let the waves wash away the attack that could have been much worse for the naïve nymph. When she starts to shiver Arianna takes her back up on the beach and finds her clothes. Arianna pulls her close and holds her tight, happy that her own body is warmer than the blood flowing through her veins.

She remembers the couple further up the beach. She remembers their fire. Maybe they've left. The cove should still be warm. It's almost dawn now and Arianna needs to get somewhere safe. But she can't just abandon the woman she's just rescued. They head for the cove.

Thankfully it's empty. The fire still burns slightly. Arianna takes her own clothes off and pulls the woman closer after taking her dress off again. Her tingle reappears, and she wants to touch her. She does. She is gentle and focused on making the woman feel good. She wants her to forget the earlier part of the evening and wake from her stunned state thinking she had drank too much. Arianna kisses her, testing for permission. The kiss is returned. Permission granted.

She moves them as close to the fire as possible. After easing her onto her back Arianna's mouth is on the pussy that was almost ripped apart by savages. She kisses it and then licks it, apologizing for her kind. The cunt tastes as good as any bad man's blood. Arianna's tongue goes inside it and there is the most sensuous moaning. This is going to be the most beautiful dream she has ever had.

The sun has started to come up outside and Arianna pauses just to be sure of the reach of its rays. When she is sure that she is safe she goes back to eating out the delicious cunt. She sucks on it for hours, knowing that the stun from those bastard's vibrations takes a while to wear off. And this poor thing got a double dose at close range. Arianna brings her to orgasm after delicious orgasm, rubbing her own clit and cunt so that she too has a few. This is how a woman should be treated. And until men realize that, Arianna will keep sticking her fangs in their bastard necks, or ripping their fucking heads off...whatever it takes!

CHAPTER 2

THE PRICE for her head must be quite high because Italy is suddenly flooded with vampires. Arianna knows that it's time to leave Europe. The Leadership is really pissed off now. She knows this because even some of their personal guard has been sent to eliminate this problem that she has become. But before she leaves Italy, there is just one final piece of business that she has in this beautiful village perched perfectly between mountain and sea.

The mayor's house is quite an elaborate piece of Tuscan art when compared to the modest dwellings around it. It even has fancy gas lamps burning in the garden. It is about as modern a work of architecture as Arianna has seen in the surrounds. This is a little difficult for her, since the lighting in and around the house lights it up like a beacon, catching the shadows of everything from vampires to rodents. But she is patient, knowing that the lamps only burn until a little after midnight. She perches herself on the roof of the house and waits.

Inside his home, the mayor is at it again. He has his third pitcher of wine while his wife exhausted already but unable to go to bed until her husband is ready, waits on him hand and foot. The staff too is still awake, the mayor enjoying the fact that the staff can be witness to his humiliation of his wife. He is really one of those people who let their power go to their heads along with their drink.

When the servants leave the house to deal with the lamps in the garden Arianna is relieved. She wants to get this over with. The lady of the house will not have to go through this shit another night. But Rita will have to meet Arianna halfway. If she doesn't, then this could go horribly wrong and she could be accused of killing her husband; something that will see her put to death as well.

"I can help you," Arianna tells Rita when she finds her alone in her room, preparing for her husband.

"Nobody can help me..." Rita sounds defeated, answering Arianna before realizing that this strange woman shouldn't be in her bedroom.

"I can help you..." Arianna says it again, this time making sure that Rita understands who and what she is, baring her fangs and lifting off the ground.

Rita's instinct is to scream. But then she realizes what Arianna is offering and she holds her own hand to her mouth.

The two decide that Arianna will make it look like a heart attack. So Rita will have to go through the entire ambit of fucking her husband, just one more time. It is going to have to be done at the time of his orgasm. Fortunately for both of them, the mayor has never slept one night without fucking the shit out of his pretty young wife.

Despite his age and his drinking, his cock has never failed to rise to the occasion either. This is not surprising. Rita is a beautiful woman in her thirties, while the husband is an extremely unattractive, toad-like man in his fifties. So the mayor is really ass-first in the butter, and his Napoleon complex is on steroids. He didn't even need to offer that big a dowry to Rita's father for this delicate perfection.

When he walks in he pulls the cord that holds his regal robe on. He is naked underneath it. He's been walking around his house with nothing hiding his fat self except for his silk gown. It took a lot of silk to make this gown.

Rita is still a little white-faced, and cannot believe that there is a vampire in her bedroom, somewhere. And she cannot believe that this evil thing has come to save her from hell. All Rita has to do is stomach being fucked by this ogre one last time. And put on one hell of a show when he is suddenly dead on top of her.

"Come here..." The mayor calls Rita to him. He looks a strange orange and pink in the lamplight. His face though is an absolute crimson. He rubs his balls, his cock hanging soft over his hand, dangling as he disturbs it. Rita knows what he wants. It's the same every night. Her mouth must warm his cock and get it hard.

"Suck it...slowly...suck it...make him stand..." He instructs her to get his cock ready for her cunt. She takes it into her mouth and moves her lips over it. She sucks on him the way he likes it. His erection develops rapidly and soon enough Rita is sucking on a hard, long tool that looks out of place on this unhealthy man.

He takes her off his cock and strokes it himself as he goes to the bed. She follows him, the worst part of their fucking ritual coming up next. The mayor gets on the bed and crouches like a tiger. He is still playing with his impressive erection. Rita comes up behind him and parts his flabby ass. It's a fucking humungous ass. She forces it apart and then sticks her head between it. Her husband moans with glee as she licks between his crack and then on his asshole directly.

"That's right Rita, right there. Get your tongue all the way in there. Lick it good..." The mayor pulls gently on his dick, loving the feeling of a tongue on his asshole... "Very good, clean it good Rita..." She hates him most for this.

Eventually, he is satisfied that she has done well on his bottom. He instructs her to get underneath him and to turn onto her stomach. After a bit of a struggle, she is in the position he wants. He pulls her hips toward

him and searches for her asshole with his dick. He forces himself down on her every time he thinks he has found it but misses. When he eventually finds it, Rita lets out a scream and he takes a hand to her mouth, whispering, "You know this is what you want. You want this. Tell me how badly you want this...Tell me..." Fortunately, Rita actually loves being fucked in the ass, always has.

When she says the words he starts fucking her hard. The intensity of his fucking is as much from his cock as it is from his weight. Rita finds it hard to breathe but she doesn't say anything. It won't help anyway. He is going to fuck her hard and he is going to fuck her long and he is not even going to care if she has an orgasm or not. As far as he is concerned, this is his wife, he has given her everything, and she should be honored that the mayor's dick is gracing her asshole with its presence.

He goes into her ass harder and harder. The sweat from his face and belly drops like rain on Rita's back. She has never allowed herself until now to be completely disgusted with this man. She hates him. Everything about him makes her want to kill herself. But her family needed the money.

Her father needed the status. And at least after he is dead, Rita will be left a rich woman. She will also be a free woman. She closes her eyes and imagines that one of the strapping stable hands, and not this bastard was fucking her. She finds her clit with her fingers and goes to the places that make her cum. One thing about the mayor though, he's got some pretty decent dick.

Arianna watches. She waits for her moment. This is a good position, because if he dies while fucking her in her ass like this then everyone will know that Rita had nothing to do with killing him, except maybe making him so excited with her delicious asshole that he keeled over and died. But everyone knows the mayor drinks too much. And he eats too much. So this isn't an unexpected death.

With the mayor completely absorbed in the pleasure he is giving himelf, and Rita's face hidden in the pillows so that she can have her own fantasies, Arianna makes her way over them. She hovers on top of the mayor and watches him rolling around over Rita. Arianna admires the woman's longsuffering. She watches, waiting. She wants to kill him at the moment of his ecstasy when his cock will be fully extended inside Rita and spilling semen into her. This will be the woman's alibi.

The mayor starts to moan, signaling his closeness. "I've got something for you..." He tells her. He promises Rita an ass full of semen as he pumps harder and harder. So caught up is he that he doesn't even notice as Arianna comes down closer so that her shadow fills the room thanks to the position of the lamp. He pumps deeper and deeper, going full might into Rita's ass. His dick pulsates, his balls contract, and his seed shoots into the hole he has been digging for himself. He lets out a loud scream, cursing so that he is heard through most of the house, complimenting his wife's nakedness so explicitly that they may as well open the door for the servants to see.

But then he is silent; a hand over his mouth and nose so he can't breathe. He struggles on top of Rita, who doesn't look up at Arianna's order. The mayor fights for his life but Arianna is strong. She stops him from breathing until he stops struggling. His cock is still lodged deep inside Rita. Then Arianna lets him drop onto his wife. She wishes Rita well and makes her way out the window. Rita takes a deep breath and then lets out a spine-chilling scream. Arianna's work here is done.

When Arianna arrives in England she finds it a hot mess. Over and above the Plague, which has brought Christians and heathens alike to their knees, there is the supernatural threat, the vampires, and the werewolves. For some reason the werewolves find London and its surrounds to be prime for feeding. This is probably because the population is weakened by hunger and disease. At least the poor are. But the majority of them are poor.

Poor people also have a lot of sex, which means a lot of babies, which means a lot of food.

She isn't particularly fond of werewolves. They are large and hairy and damp. They smell too. But it's a strange, sour smell that Arianna has never been able to place. Wet dogs smell like wet dogs. Werewolves smell like something else altogether. Arianna makes a note to herself to avoid a run-in with them. She will lay low in the city for a while, losing herself among the lost and forgotten. She hates that she arrived after the Ripper had left. That's one man she would have loved to sink her teeth into.

The streets are filthy. And Arianna is hungry. But looking at the people all she feels is sympathy. She moves past the strange looks trying to get a sense of where she might get a meal. There are a lot of miserable women. But misery is just everywhere so it's difficult to zone in on which of it is man-made. Everyone strains to get a closer look at Arianna. She realizes that it's the way she is dressed. She's clearly not from here. A corpse in an alley provides her with the change of clothes she needs, another whore who succumbed to the cold but an hour earlier.

Now she moves among the people like one of them. Even when a few ladies of the night recognize the dress they just shake their heads and say a silent prayer for their deceased colleague. Arianna feels for these people who simply have no choice but to accept this fate, while another part of London is partying late into the night in grand rooms, heated by grand fires and imported wines. Unused roasts are fed to dogs while the bulk of the population has resorted to eating dogs or being eaten by them. This isn't a world for human beings. Not any more...

The smoke from the coal fires in the city seems to settle most on the poor. Arianna needs some fresh air and so she makes her way to where the streets are cleaner and the houses better. Just a few streets in and even the smell of waste disappears. This city is clearly designed for the rich. But it won't be long before the poor take it back. Arianna has seen this happen so often in the last couple of hundred years.

She picks up on the sounds of sex. In the part of town, she's just come from people are fucking in the streets, finding comfort between each other's legs. Some find corners, and some couldn't be bothered. She looks around her at the impressive houses. There are lights on in some of the windows. She peeps in. Again she is disgusted at this opulence so close to such poverty. These people make love and fuck and play and drink and eat with not a care in the world.

Then she hears it; the sound of giggling and laughter and promise. She remembers the couple from the beach in Italy, and despite her need to feed she floats in the direction of this pair. It's a grand house, with the remainder of a party downstairs. On the second story, there are lots of bedrooms, lots of drunk people sleeping everywhere but the beds. She goes to the other side of the house and finds what she is looking for. It's chilly and she wishes she was inside. But she will have to be happy with her view through the window.

"Let me see that beautiful body...please..." A young man, twenty maybe, is begging a woman to take off her clothes.

"That's all you ever want. What about your promise? I can't go on like this...We can't go on like this..." She is almost distraught in her attempts to make him understand how serious she is.

"I know...I know... I'll tell my parents soon, then we'll marry...and then you'll be completely free from your life on the streets...I promise...Now take off this dress..."

She is forlorn, having heard this a thousand times. It's always the same with him. The woman insists they leave for a far place where the burden of her past life as a prostitute won't haunt her. He agrees, tugging carelessly at her dress.

Finally, the woman relents. She allows herself to believe his promises again, allowing him to take her clothes off until she stands naked in the dimly lit room. He walks around her, examining her beauty, the kind that is too innocent for one so tainted. Soon both of them are naked and the man takes hold of his woman from the back, letting their bodies fuse. It's clear on his face that he wants her. She wants him too, but not just for this.

His hands move onto her breasts and he rubs them. He pulls on her nipples a little too hard and she reprimands him for being drunk. He whispers his love for her and then moves his hands down her belly while kissing her neck and rubbing his cock against the softness of her ass. Then his hands come together on her cunt and he plays with the soft hair there. He fiddles around on her clit and then the tip of a finger disappears into her pussy. He plays with her hole, pulling her harder against him, still kissing her neck and then her back.

He turns her to face him and then places her hand on his cock. She needs two hands to move up and down the gigantic erection on her skinny lover. His balls are massive too and with both her hands she moves delicately over cock and balls. He eases her down so that she is squatting. He wills his dick into her mouth and watches as she sucks on most of it. He holds her head in place and helps her to take more by thrusting gently into her. Occasionally she pushes him back because he has gone too deep. He apologizes but then makes the same mistake over and over again.

She hates it when he's drunk. She tells him this. He is suddenly impatient and annoyed. He pulls her to her feet, trying to keep the softness in his eyes. But Arianna, watching him more than her, can see through his act, through his lies, through the mask that will just ensure that he gets some pussy tonight. But this isn't a crime. This isn't something that she can kill a man for. All men do it. And besides, despite her irritation, the woman is enjoying it, the smell of her wet pussy seeping through the slit that is left by the window that hasn't been closed properly.

The couple moves to the bed and the woman is mounted. He moves her legs apart and inserts his cock. She holds onto his shoulders as he goes deep. He moves around on her to adjust himself and then he is all the way inside her. She tries to hold him back a little, needing as she always does, to warm up just a little. But he is out of patience and fucks her while telling her that it will feel good in a minute. She gives him his minute and then it starts to feel fantastic.

Arianna watches them fucking. She moves from tingling all over to tuning in to the sounds around her. She is going to have to eat before dawn. There must be something around here somewhere, or else she's going to have to take her chances in the slums. She watches as the woman has an orgasm and then the man. He keeps fucking her a little while longer until he is sure that he can't pull another round from his cock just yet. Too much wine will do that. He holds her for a minute and tells her to sleep, that he'll be right back.

Arianna is about to leave, happy with the night's entertainment. But something inside her keeps her watching the woman on the bed. Something isn't right. The woman is trying to move herself to a comfortable position but she is struggling. She can't feel herself. Could she be drunk? Arianna knows she can't be, or she wouldn't have been annoyed by her lying lover's drunkenness.

Then the door opens again and the twenty-year-old is back. He is accompanied by two other men, about his age. They laugh and joke about the opiate they always slip into her drink. They joke about how she never knows that each night she is here she gets three dicks for the price of one.

The lover pulls on his cock until it is firm again and he mounts the woman who is now chasing the dragon. He fucks her hard but can't cum. His friends are already pulling on their own cocks, readying themselves for a ride. Lover-boy keeps fucking until his mates have solid erections. Arianna is livid. She watches this, wishing they were outside, wishing they were drunker so that she doesn't struggle with them. She wishes that the four policemen on horses just beyond the wall would fuck off.

She leaves the window and moves around the house quickly, looking through the windows, getting a sense of where everyone is and how many people are awake. There are a few men in the parlor, drinking and playing a card game. There's some fucking but it's lazy and consensual. Mostly everyone has passed out. Some of the staff is hovering around in case the lords need assistance. Arianna needs a way into this house and into the bedroom upstairs so that she can sort out those three cunts that are probably already going to town inside that poor woman.

And boy are they going at it. The woman is unaware of who is on her, lost in the drug. She is enjoying herself, sure that it is her man inside her. Even when there is a cock in her ass and one in her pussy she is sure that it is one cock. The men really give her a solid working, as they have done many times before, and fill her with their seed before Arianna manages to get back up to the window. But she is glad that she didn't act hastily because now the three fuckers are smoking on a pipe of their own; a post pussy celebration. They are soon lost in their own worlds, hallucinating separately but together, still rubbing their satisfied dicks.

Arianna wastes no time. She slides the window up as slowly as she can. It's moments like this that she wishes vampires could walk through walls. As soon as all their eyes are closed she slips into the room and hovers high above them. She knows that she will have very little time from the first neck to the last, any screaming probably filling the room quickly. She has another idea.

She gets her clothing off, all off, and hangs the stolen

dress on the chandelier. Then she lowers herself silently so that she is standing behind them. Then she manages her most sultry tone and greets them, welcoming them to paradise. The three pass the pipe around one more time and then check with each other that they all see the naked raven-haired woman with inviting thighs and delicious-looking cunt. They are in agreement that they all see her, passing the pipe around yet again. Arianna sits herself among them.

They touch her hungrily, the woman on the bed forgotten. Arianna moves her fingers along all three dicks, rock hard and ready to go. These are nice cocks. Just a pity the men they come with. She moves her mouth onto their meat, one at a time, sucking slowly, lulling them further into the dream they aren't sure they're having. Her fingers, the tips of her nails, run along their balls, and these men are in paradise. Someone dubs her Eve and himself Adam, so Arianna takes his hand and places it on her Garden of Eden. She lets them move their fingers in and out of her pussy which has become quite wet.

Soon enough the men want to fuck her. They pull her and push her among themselves, all of them wanting to go first. Arianna isn't about to let them inside her cunt. She grabs one and pulls him close, then runs her mouth over his cock again. She eases her fangs into his erection so that he isn't surprised by the sting. He warns her to be careful with her teeth but not too careful, the pain is good. She moves on to the other cocks, giving them the same sensuous bite. In seconds the three are writhing on the floor, turning. Arianna won't let that happen.

As they lose consciousness, she is on their cocks again. This time she isn't shooting her poison into them. She is sucking hard on their dicks, her teeth deeply embedded in the tissues, finding veins, drinking her dinner. She enjoys the taste of cock and blood, it's an interesting cocktail. There are traces of semen too which she doesn't mind. A little semen is good for her hair. She hadn't realized just how hungry she was. By the time she leaves the room, the sleeping woman in her arms, she has left the men looking dried up and mummified.

For as long as she can she flies over the city with the woman in her arms. But as soon as the dark, dingy part of town she is now in starts to teem with a life she is on the ground. She looks like a whore helping another drunken whore home. So nobody pays them any mind. Arianna manages to find an inn where the keeper will take a blowjob for a room. She sucks on his filthy cock, bringing him to a climax quick enough. A moment later she has laid the woman in the bed, having scrubbed her down, and leaves her to sleep.

In the forest, Arianna is desperate for a dark place. She seeks out the hollows of the trees, but the light of the moon seeps through, meaning that the sun will probably do the same when dawn comes. And dawn is fast approaching. Arianna is tired inside, but physically she can keep moving. She doesn't want to, and finally finds a deep hollow under an ancient oak that looks like it will work.

In the dark, she remembers some of the conversations she heard on the streets in London. The vampires have been here. They're probably still here. But the werewolves are what the people fear. They, unlike the vampires, rip their victims to shreds. When the werewolves are out feeding, the agonizing screams of the victims fill the night like the black. With vampires, your neck is broken and your blood is drained. The people appreciate this courtesy that makes funerals easier, allowing loved ones the last rights to view and bid farewell to their dead. With werewolves you bury pieces. And, chances are, not all the pieces.

Arianna is asleep for two days. She has mastered the art of closing her eyes and dreaming. If only she could master the things she dreamed. The darkness is thick when she stirs from her hole, the forest quiet; too quiet. She moves just off the forest floor so as not to disturb the silence. But the fact that she cannot hear a creature stir bothers her. Where have they gone? Why have they gone?

Her questions are answered quickly enough. She comes out of the far end of the woods and into a clearing. She is overcome by the smell of death. These humans on the ground have been dead for days. This explains why she hadn't picked up on it. Before she can be sad about it she hears a thud and looks to where the sound is coming from. A young man is surrounded by a pack of wolves that tower almost double over him. He is going at them with everything he's got. Everything, in this case, is a large stick. It's not even making a dent.

The werewolves play with him. They come in, scratch at him, and then step back. It's clear that they are in no hurry to kill him. He curses them under his breath, his words barely audible from exhaustion. He points to the women on the floor, wanting to know from the wolves if there are no women in hell. They growl back, also under their breaths, mocking him, telling him that hell's whores don't taste so good. They tell him that the warmth between human thighs is irresistible.

Arianna wonders at the similarity between wolf and vampire. They are very different to look at but come with the same bad attitude and blatant disregard for life. She looks at the naked women on the floor, dead, and realizes that this man probably followed the wolves into the forest in the hope of saving them. And now that he knows that he is too late to save them, like her, he has resolved to punish the wolves. He is putting up a valiant fight. But it's a fight that it is obvious he is going to eventually lose once the wolves tire of their game.

She walks out of the wood and into the clearing. The moon catches her in all her splendor and the wolves look up, only now picking up her scent. They know what she is and start to bark at her. Then they growl menacingly, "we know who you are, witch..."

She knows they do, and tells them that much. Her confidence pisses them off. And after smacking the young man to the ground to be finished up later, they descend on Arianna.

Tanner is barely conscious from the blow. But he is curious as to the conversation he's just heard between the wolves and this woman. So he struggles to keep his eyes open and see for himself why she is more important to them than he. What do they mean when they say they know who she is? Who is she?

Arianna grabs the first two dogs to reach her and carries them high up in the night sky. She moves so high that she disappears for a second. Then the two dogs fall like buildings back to the ground. They jerk for a minute but then are dead. The others circle her, salivating as they contemplate bringing an end to this vampire, and earning favor with The Leadership. It's not a bad thing to be owed a favor by The Leadership, even for a wolf.

A couple of wolves pounce but miss. Arianna is juiced from her recent feed and the rest she got. She moves like lightning between them as they try to grab hold of her. Their efforts are futile and she succeeds in wearing them out. They heave now as they try to catch their breaths and regain their strength. But werewolves are large and heavy.

So while they have the power, they just don't have the stamina.

Tanner can't believe his eyes as one by one Arianna picks off these dogs. She snaps their necks loudly and rips their heads off. This isn't necessary but she enjoys it, looking at the women she was too late to save. She can't keep losing lives like this. But she also can't be everywhere at once. And she has to stop being so fucking sensitive. For a second she tells herself that she's only human. But reminds herself as she brings the last wolf to a painful end with a rapid wrist movement that this really isn't so.

She sits on the ground, taking stock of this scene. Arianna slows her breath and calms herself. She's done her best. She looks to where Tanner is still lying on the ground. He's not dead. But he's also barely alive. She goes over to him to inspect the damage. This is bad. It's worse than even Tanner thinks it is because he is looking at her with wide eyes, introducing himself casually, and then warning her that he too now knows what she is. He reaches weakly for his stick, threatening her not to touch him.

But the battle has taken its toll on him and for all his gallantry, he passes out. Arianna is tempted to leave him where he is, to let him bleed into peace and eternity. But he's got gentle eyes and a strong face. He also has a very good heart and this is deserving of saving. She takes the man in her arms and moves through the night toward the city, this time flying high above the trees in the forest to avoid running into more wolves.

She is clever about taking him to the right hospital. Arianna finds a nobleman patrolling the streets as they do, looking for a taste of the exotic that resides only in the forbidden parts. She presents herself as a street woman and after luring him into an alley, she relieves him of his clothing. With her clothes back on, and Tanner now dressed like a nobleman, Arianna rips the clothing such that they are conducive to his wounds.

The staff at the hospital receives the unconscious man they presume to be a lord eagerly. In his pockets, Arianna finds the money for the deposit and then leaves the rest with the nurse to be given to Tanner when he is mended. She keeps some for herself, English money a handy thing to have in England. She leaves the hospital amid whispers of what a man like that was doing with a woman like her, and why he would risk taking her to the forest instead of one of the local inns if he wanted to fuck her so badly. But then Arianna remembers her dress, stolen from a whore, and she forgives them for their questions...

CHAPTER 3

THE NURSES WORK on getting Tanner's clothes off. They need to clean him and prep him for the doctors. There is a huge gash on his thigh that requires that they remove all his clothes, even his underwear. This is just a part of their job and they do it professionally. But they still can't help but admire his cock.

As they work on him with their sponges both women avoid getting to his cock even though they want to, and have to because of all the blood. The doctors are already scrubbing up outside and ready to go to work. Eventually, they go at it together and they get Tanner scrubbed up and cleaned up to avoid the onset of infection. The doctors come in and work on him for most of the night, stitching him up and cleaning stray objects lodged in practically every part of him. There are a few broken ribs and a dislocated shoulder that need attention.

Then the nurses wheel him to a private room for important patients. This is where he will recover. They get him some hospital pajamas and a gown and set about their postoperative cleaning and dressing so that the patient is comfortable. Tanner is not aware of anything happening around him, his blood is filled with the anesthetic and tons of morphine. The women know this, and they allow their curiosity to get the better of them.

"Now that's the kind of cock you don't see every day on an Englishman..." Clara, the Irish nurse is always quick to bring down the English...

"I'll bet not even on most Irishman..." Ethel, the English nurse counters her attempted insult, in support of her countrymen.

With Tanner naked now on his bed they work him over with warm sponges. This time they are not so shy about his cock and since there is no urgency, they take their time. Nobody will come into the room, knowing that the assigned nurses are busy with the patient. But just in case, Clara locks the door. Ethel looks at her with eyes filled with mischief. This pair loves working together, especially when the patient is a man, and especially when the surgery has been heavy and he is out for the count. They make sure that they give Tanner a thorough sponge bath before they play so that they don't waste too much time after.

Clara takes off her panties and puts them in her pocket. Ethel does the same. They check to see that none of Tanner's bandages are showing signs of ruptured stitching. They're not. The doctors have done a good job on him. You really did get what you paid for in England these days. Clara takes Tanner's dick between her fingers, holding it at the tip and then pulling it up so that is straight.

"There's enough here to give a cunt a decent enough stuffing I reckon..." She speaks as though there was no way in the world that Tanner could hear her. They admire its length as it takes three hands to cover the length of the shaft. Granted, the women have small hands, but still.

For a moment they play with Tanner's soft meat but soon realize that it will be easier to play with if it was a little wet. It will also be easier to get it to stiffen up, which is ultimately what they want. The Irish woman goes onto it with her mouth, her friend upset that she was slow on the approach. She watches as her friend's mouth fills with cock, and then watches as she slides her mouth up so that the cock is free. Then she is on the cock again, sucking it inside her mouth as though it tasted like ice cream.

Not to be outdone, the English woman goes around the other side and starts licking his balls. The sack is huge and soft and warm, but the balls inside it are firm. These are a hardworking man's balls. The nurses work on every part of Tanner's sexuality in silence. Their mouths are as good a team as they are, and Tanner soon has a massive erection that he is essentially not even aware of. Now the Irish woman sucks him with gusto as her friend comes around to her, gets between her legs, and starts to eat out the pussy covered in soft orange curls.

Then Ethel's fingers are inside Clara so that the woman doing the fingering can watch the sucking. She is also fingering herself as she goes. Tanner isn't making a sound. They can only hope that he can feel them on his dick and that it makes him feel a lot better after his little run-in with death. After she has sucked him so that her jaw hurts, and after she has had a climax thanks to the fingering in her pussy, Clara gives her friend the cock.

Thin lips slide over Tanner's meat and he is again being sucked off. This mouth is deeper and his entire cock is inside it. It fits comfortably. The redhead is now on her friend with her fingers, going hard and deep but also not too eagerly. She also touches her own clit, thanking it for the climax. Ethel raises her leg onto the table so that her friend's fingers can go all the way up inside her. She aches for maximum penetration. If it wasn't for his injuries, she would be riding the shit out of Tanner's dick right this minute.

But this isn't necessary as she has an incredible orgasm. She keeps sucking Tanner, wanting to taste what he's hiding in his balls. She sucks for another hour before he finally shoots into her mouth. She swallows as much of it as possible before her friend too comes up and laps up the left-overs. She is really grateful even for this little bit that she has left. They lick him a few more times and even kiss him on his lips. Then they kiss his dick and suck it some more even though it is now soft. They finger themselves and each other the whole time and only put their panties back on after their third orgasm.

When they leave Tanner he lies still for the remainder of the night. There is still no sign of movement the next day, but he is alive. So the nurses keep an eye on him and go about their duties. The hospital is very busy during the day so there is no chance of a repeat of last night's escapade. They are on duty today and nothing else.

The doctor checks in on his patient often, especially when it seems that Tanner might be coming out of his sleep. But he is restless, and they take the decision to restrain him on the bed just to protect him from himself. It seems that whatever it is that attacked him in real life is now chasing him in his dreams. Tanner opens his eyes once or twice, he isn't sure where he is, and then is back asleep. They give him some more morphine for the pain that he has no way of saying he is feeling. The doctor orders that a nurse be in the room with him at all times now in case he wakes up.

The sweat on his brow gives some indication of the intensity of the dreams in his head. Whatever he is running from must really have him racing. The nurse looks up from her embroidery to Tanner each time he moves or makes a sound. She gives it a minute and when he is resting again, she lets it go and gets back to the work of her fingers. She can only guess at the horrors. But Tanner is dreaming of no horrors. His head is filled with fantasies of the dark-haired woman who saved his life.

Tanner is back in the clearing, with no sign of the wolves. All he sees is Arianna, naked, at the mouth of the cave. He goes toward her and she disappears into the cave. He follows her into the darkness, unsure but fearless.

Inside the cave is a warm, roaring fire in the back. There are blankets on the floor and Arianna is already lying on them, running her fingers over her naked body, inviting him to join her.

Arianna helps Tanner get naked and then places her lips on his. He kisses her deeply. With his body on hers, the kisses intensify. Tanner takes full control of the situation, choosing the best route to make beautiful love to this mysterious woman. He kisses her neck and then her mouth again. He rubs his face against hers as he moves his hairy chest over hers. He can already feel the warmth from her pussy on his balls as he moves back and forth over it.

Then he puts her nipples in his mouth. He sucks on them as though he expects the waters of life to come up out of them and into his mouth. His mouth is warm, as warm as Arianna's body. Everything about her begs to be made love to. Tanner looks at her perfect face and wants to do just that. He kisses down her belly and plays with her naval using his tongue. Her legs bend at the knee and her feet plant themselves flat on the blankets.

Then Tanner is blowing gently into the curls covering her cunt. He blows harder on her clit and then gently again over the surface of her vagina. His mouth comes into contact with her clit and he gives it the softest kisses. Then his tongue is on it and Arianna's clit claps with joy. Tanner licks it a little harder and then searches for her slit with his tongue.

He sends the tip into her, finding the entrance warm and wet. He uses a finger to part the pussy a little so that he can look into it. His cock yearns for this cunt now. But he wants to taste a little more of her first. He laps up the moisture on the surface of her snatch. And then he moves his tongue into her pussy slowly. Arianna moans loudly and tries to tie herself in a knot as Tanner continues his determined mission to please her.

Tanner's tongue moves all the way inside her cunt now so that his lips are resting in the curls there. His nose breathes in the aromas coming from her clit. He eats her pussy out with the appreciation of a child who's just been given the first slice of a freshly baked loaf of bread. This is all he wants and the only place he wants to be. The fire roars to the rhythm of Arianna's drum.

When Tanner comes up again he finds her eyes closed and smiling. He plants his lips on her smile and her mouth opens to receive his tongue. They kiss while Tanner finds the inside of Arianna's cunt with his extraordinary cock. The heat inside her pussy is as extraordinary. This is the moment that he has been building her for. And it is everything he had hoped it would be.

He sucks her tongue into his mouth and plays with it using his. He doesn't want to lose the taste of her on his lips. His dick moves all the way up inside her and then pauses to draw into itself all of her fires. Then it is coming out in a smooth stroke so that it is running against her walls and stoking the fire it will dive back into in a minute. When he goes back in he finds the furnace raging. Again he lingers in the lava before pulling out slowly to re-stoke Arianna's oven.

They make love for an eternity, and Tanner feels the beginning of his orgasm. Arianna's pussy is dripping from all of hers. He has given her many. She has appreciated each one. And he has appreciated being the one giving them to her. His own eyes close as he thrusts gently into her over and over toward the end.

But then the room fills with a smell that isn't the fire. He pulls his mouth off of Arianna's as it suddenly tastes like his mouth is stuffed with dead vermin. Arianna's eyes are open and so is her mouth as she screams for him to fuck her harder. "Fuck me, Fuck me, Fuck me..." she screams. Her tone is vile, the words falling from her lips like vomit. She screams over and over again, "fuck me, fuck me, fuck me..."

Tanner tries to pull his cock from this witch. But she grabs him hard and holds him where he is. She opens her mouth to reveal perfectly positioned fangs, and then she goes for his neck...

The nurse tries in vain to wake him. Tanner is convulsing and burning with fever. Two doctors come into the room and try but he will not open his eyes. They inject him with a sedative and hold him down. Tanner has almost yanked the restraints from the bed's railing. It takes a moment but soon the sedative kicks in and he is jerking mildly before not moving at all. The nurse is a little shaken but the doctors tell her that it is normal for patients who've just experienced trauma to have nightmares. The nurse knows this, but still, she is glad when her replacement arrives to take the next two-hour shift.

Arianna has found refuge from the day in the local mausoleum. She hates it but has no choice. Sometimes she wishes she was like other vampires who liked this death shit.

But she isn't. It's the curse of being turned. There's something inside you that nags at you when you were once living to die and now you're killing to live. She knows it isn't right. Well not really. But a woman's got to eat. And at least she is selective about who she eats.

The sun sets at last and she stirs from the stone cell. Walking through the cemetery and among the graves she wishes it was her under the ground, resting for eternity. Immortality is a restless existence. At the best of times, all you're doing is wandering. Sometimes it seems that the world takes too long to change and so there is very little to excite you. Mortals really don't appreciate how good they've got it.

Shadows all around her let her know that she is not alone. She finds the freshest grave and sits on it. Vampires smell like death to other vampires. So Arianna hopes that being so close to a rotting corpse will hide her scent. It does, and the vampires make off. She gives them a short lead and then follows, knowing what they have come out to do. Their appetites are really insatiable.

Again she is in the wrong part of town. She watches as the vampires land in the darkness, walking among the humans casually as though they were themselves human. Arianna doesn't recognize any of them, six handsome devils on a mission. The six enter the red light district, although, the entire town seems to be a red-light district. She is going to have to move very quickly.

Arianna watches as an Armenian woman steps out of the shadows and into the path of two vampires. "I can make you very happy for a small fee..." she says, as she summons the pair into her little corner of the street.

"No doubt you can...and will..." they are amused that

she has no idea what she has brought upon herself in her naivety.

The pair smiles at each other and goes to her. All three disappear into the shadows. The streets are a buzz and Arianna doesn't know if it is going to be possible to avoid a scene. The woman is going to scream if she realizes what she has called upon herself. She will definitely scream if Arianna just rocks up and pulls the heads off the shoulders of the men whose money she wants in her purse after their dicks are done in her pussy.

There won't be time for her to wait for the sleeper vibration to do its thing. Arianna can smell it. The woman's cunt already smells from earlier sex. So the vampires are already aroused by this odor, wanting to add their own blend to it. Arianna gets as close as she can and waits, watching as they lift the woman's skirt over her head and reveal her cunt. With the woman's face covered she cannot see the fangs that are already protruding in anticipation of the main course. But first the appetizer...

Both vampires get on their knees and lick her pussy together with their long tongues. She is spreading her legs wide, not expecting this treatment on her cunt. Men usually just arrive and shove their cocks inside her. And five minutes later she is paid and it is over. But these two are licking her and playing with her cunt so that for the first time her pussy is wet all on its own. Then fingers move into her, two, then five. This is too much. She tries to pull the skirt off her face but then one of them is holding it in place, rubbing her breasts so that she is again lulled by this tenderness. But the fist in her cunt is stretching her so that her head hurts.

Then it is out, ripped from inside her. There is a moment of uncertainty but then she wants it back in. The vampires swop and the other one has his fingers filling her. He too gets up to a whole hand and fists her for a while. Again she wants to get the skirt off her face because she can't breathe now. But they won't allow it.

"Relax, don't struggle. It will be easier if you don't fight. There's a little extra if you take it like a good little whore..." She doesn't know who has spoken, only that the tone makes her think of the devil. The promise of extra money has her resign herself to this intense action inside her cunt. It's not unpleasant action. But this is her first time.

Arianna sees an opportunity, but it won't work unless the vampires are distracted and she has the advantage of surprise. With her head covered, the prostitute won't see her. But when she goes for one vampire, the other one will. He will let the other vampires in the area know where she is. This could turn into a blood bath. Arianna will have to wait until they are fucking her, seeing from the way they are positioning her now that they will go in together, one in front and one at the back. She's going to have to be swift; this young woman doesn't look like she can handle more than a dozen vampire strokes.

She watches as they take out their dicks. Both of them have curved veiny cocks. They are thick and long too. What is it about vampires and big dicks? It really seems unnecessary. Arianna feels for the woman who is begging them to go slowly. The vampires are not patient lovers though and both of them ram into her at once. She is about to yell out but a hand finds her mouth over the skirt. She exhales hard as the two start to thrust. Despite the wetness of her pussy and the beating in her clit, she senses that the dicks inside her are not quite right. The Armenian has heard stories. And the coldness filling her with every stroke lets her know that she is in trouble.

Arianna descends on the trio. Before he can speak she has broken the neck of the vampire fucking the woman's pussy. She goes for the other one second only because it's a little harder to pull a thick cock from an ass than it is to escape from a cunt. His neck snaps quickly. Arianna pulls both men from their respective holes and flies off with her kill as the woman struggles to free her face from her skirt. She runs into the light and tries not to look shaken. Already she is worried about the money that would have paid her rent for a week.

Arianna finds a deserted alley and tears the heads of the pair. She is worried as the air fills with the smell of fear from every direction that she won't get to the other four vampires in time. But she is going to have to try. The entire area stinks of sex and pheromones and cock and so it is hard for Arianna to know where to go until the vampires add themselves to the mix. And when they do, she moves quickly in the direction where this smell is strongest.

In an attic in one of the boarding houses, two women are tied to a bed. Their clothing is on the floor, and the man they don't know is a vampire yet circling the bed, stroking his dick.

"Very impressive, isn't it?" The vampire runs his hand up and down on his cock so that the women can process just how big it is. "You want it?"

He gets onto the bed between the two who are both begging him to put his dick in their mouths. He settles comfortably between them and just sends his fingers into both of them at the same time instead. The women moan loudly.

"Aah, warm and deep. Such inviting little pussies you have..." He continues to finger them while telling all the things he envisages doing with them. Their cunts become wetter and wetter as they imagine these things. Their pussies heat up as his fingers go deeper into them. The pair is soon fucking into the air as soon as he removes his fingers to show their trick how desperate they are for his dick, and of course his money. He is happy that they are so eager to please.

But he doesn't give them dick. Instead,, he has his mouth on their cunts, eating them out with his powerful tongue. This serpent penetrates them deep. Again they are wet and find themselves yearning, aching to be fucked. This man's beauty has them super horny almost as much as the contents of his money bag.

Arianna is going insane as she watches through the window in the roof that is too small for her to get into. She will have to go through one of the others or the door. But then she will have to walk slowly, the building full and busy. Flying is not an option. There is no time to waste. She flies down off the roof and is on the street. She walks into the door and avoids the burly woman at the desk. She walks like a seasoned prostitute, as though she is coming to meet a trick. Her pace is quick up the stairs, avoiding a couple too horny to make it to the room.

The three-story house is large and dilapidated. But nobody cares. It's warm and safe, sort of. Arianna gets to the top of the stairs and gets her bearings, although the smell of the women is leading a clear path for her. She gets to the door and it's locked. There will be no surprise here. She is going to force the door open and the fight is going to be on immediately. Again she times it so that by the time she pushes the door open the vampire has his dick inside one of the women.

Arianna jumps on him just as he is thrusting into her. She pulls him up hard and he pulls his cock out of the woman much to her relief. He was really giving her cunt a beating. The humans watch as the vampires tear the already torn-up attic apart. They wonder how Arianna knew where they were, but they are grateful that she did. Both women shudder at how close they came to being dinner. Looking at Arianna though, they aren't sure if they're out of danger, her hissing and her fangs making her look every bit as threatening as the vampire she is fighting. Arianna tears his head off and it gets stuck at the spine. She forgot to break his neck. By the time she does he has sprayed blood all over her and on the floor.

When he disappears in a heap of ash, Arianna frees the women. They thank her and then run from the room. Arianna leaves the room too, knowing that the two, sisters, will already probably be telling the story now. She tries to find a bathroom but they are all occupied. The blood on her is disgusting. When she gets to the top of the stairs she knows that leaving this way is not a plan. Walking up and down the passage she hears heavy boots on the stairs. She knows that she is in shit.

She finds a room that is empty and takes her clothes off. She uses the sheets on the bed to wipe the blood from her. She checks the mirror and makes sure that she looks disheveled and that there is no blood on her that can be seen. She runs back into the passage and lets out a blood-curdling scream, yelling *vampire, vampire...* Everyone starts to file out of the rooms, most of them naked. The screaming becomes chaotic and Arianna holds the sheet wrapped around her and follows the other people running from the building, escaping from vampires that are not there anymore.

In the streets, she gets lost easily in the crowd. She is in a panic now knowing that she has lost two vampires. It's impossible for her to focus now, the streets in chaos. She has to let it go. This is her ultimate frustration. She wishes that there were more like her. If there were, they could save more women. She makes peace with this and goes off to try and find something to wear.

Back at the hospital, Tanner is burning up. His hallucinations are getting more and more intense. He is also waking up on his own often. When he is awake he is incoherent. He asks strange questions, telling them that a vampire saved him. The doctors put him out again and discuss the possibility of institutionalizing him, even just for a while. They don't doubt that he had an encounter with a vampire, but it was more likely werewolves. But the idea that either of these vile things could have saved him, he can only be delusional.

The hospital can't find any information on his family, not knowing what his last name is. And nobody is coming around looking for him. The only link to the outside world is the whore who brought him in. But he is now convinced that she is a vampire.

In his head, Tanner is again in the clearing. This time he is the one drawing Arianna to him, hungering for her. Again his dream is vivid...

Arianna doesn't resist Tanner and allows him to hold her close. They don't go into the cave. Tanner undresses them in the light of the moon. The rays of light are on their backs as they roll around in the soft earth, Tanner's cock deep inside Arianna as she moans with each of his strokes.

But then they are surrounded. A dozen evil-looking men close in on them and yank them apart. Tanner waits to be killed but instead, he watches as Arianna's neck is broken. He watches as her body falls limp in the grips of the vampire who's just snapped her neck. And then to his horror, he watches as her head is pulled off her shoulders and held up like a trophy. Her body drops to the ground and she is left to fizzle away in a haze.

Tanner jumps up and is immediately yanked down by the belts holding him on the bed. He needs to get out of here. He knows that Arianna is real, and with his dreams, there is a deep urgency inside him now to find her. He can't be sure if he is just having paranoid attachments because Arianna has saved his life. But whatever it is, he needs to get out of his restraints and go and find her.

When the last nurse for the evening comes in to check on him he pretends to be asleep. He waits for her to make adjustments to his blanket and then to run her hands up his leg as she usually does, getting too close to his dick but always saying to herself, he is sure, that she is just checking the bandages on his thigh wound. Tanner wills himself to have an erection and his cock pushes up on the hospital clothes he has on, knowing just what this will do to Clara.

Clara ties her red hair in a tighter bun and she looks at the door. She knows it isn't locked but she can't help touching Tanner's cock. Just then he opens his eyes. She is so focused on his dick that she doesn't see him watching her. She moves her hand up and down on his meat and then her cunt goes ablaze so that she loses her self-control. She goes to the door and locks it.

Tanner pretends to be sleeping again as she runs her mouth over his dick, just wanting a little taste. She is digging her finger into her pussy as she does this. When she is totally in it Tanner just waits until she has an orgasm. The blowjob isn't too bad so he can wait. She sucks on his cock for ten minutes before she is satisfied. When she straightens up she starts when she sees him watching her.

"Did you enjoy that?" Tanner asks her casually.

"Uhm, I'm sorry, I thought you were..." She can hardly speak through her embarrassment...

"...too out of it not to know that I was having my dick sucked?" Still, Tanner is casual.

"I'm sorry..." Clara looks away, truly ashamed at being found out.

"Don't be...I like your mouth on my dick. It's just a shame that I can't taste your pussy too...only seems fair, don't you think..." Tanner looks at his erection so that Clara's eyes, too, fall on his cock. She ponders the situation for just a second before removing the key from the door and putting it in her pocket.

She undoes his restraints. Tanner is on his feet, unsteady. He needs to get his balance. So he pulls off her panties and sends his cock into her just to give his feet a moment to get familiar with the ground again.

He brings her to an incredible orgasm and then kisses her as though she were the only woman in the world. She is in heaven and her concentration is lost. Tanner fucks her again, this time on the bed, just to wear her out. This time he takes all her clothes off just so that he can be sure that she won't run from the room too quickly. When he is done with her he gets up and takes the key from her pocket. He puts his robe on and wraps it around himself tight. She watches him leave, too embarrassed to draw attention to the room with her lying in the patient's bed with a wet pussy and no clothes on.

Tanner makes it to the utility part of the hospital and steals a cleaner's uniform. He makes it out of the service entrance to the hospital and stumbles along into the streets, beginning his search for the vampire who saved his life and won't get out of his head. He needs to find Arianna...

CHAPTER 4

IN THE WOODS again Arianna seeks out a different hollow. She knows that all the vampires that are in London are not just here for the cuisine. More members of the Leadership's guard are in the area. She can sense them. She has had enough encounters with them to pick up their scents easily. It's all this fighting. The more she saves lives, the more her own life is in danger. She's making a lot of enemies very fast.

Arianna is not comfortable at all tonight. For the first time in a long time, she can't bring herself to sleep. She feels like the walls, as it were, are closing in on her. If she is killed there will be nothing to stop the vampires and werewolves from just continuing to do what they want. There will be nothing to bring justice to the women and children treated so terribly by this generation of men. Arianna must keep fighting, as long as she can. She is settling into the idea of forever, at last.

Her thoughts are interrupted by the silence outside. She knows what this meant last time. She hopes it doesn't mean the same thing tonight. She stirs carefully and checks out the immediate area. Then she checks out a little further, willing herself to zone in on whoever might be in trouble. The only thing coming in on the wind is the cold. Arianna might just be a little paranoid, never before having had so many intense battles in such quick succession before. And the wolves are a burdensome bulk.

She wonders at her appetite. She isn't really hungry. She has strength sufficient for another day or two. Moving around the forest it is so quiet that she can hear herself moving through the air. It's a strange thing to hear nothing except you move. She flies around with no clear direction.

When she comes upon the same clearing where she had battled the werewolves she finds no signs of life or death. The bodies have since been carried away by scavengers. She goes closer and examines the entrance to the cave. Nothing comes back at her from inside except the vibrations of bats, her new cousins for eight hundred years.

She sits in the mouth of the cave and tries to imagine the terrible things that the women must have gone through before they were killed. She's heard that some women were actually giving themselves to the wolves sexually, promised meat from the forest that only the wolves can catch and take back to their families. Instead, the women became the meal.

She remembers Tanner and wonders at his bravery and his stupidity. But she admires him, wishing he was like her so that they could fight this fight together. But then she reprimands herself for wishing this curse on anyone else.

Then Arianna realizes that she's been reactionary for the most part. She has simply helped women in trouble wherever she was. She hasn't gone about her mission with purpose, even though she had always been clear about what she wanted to achieve. She has focused on the victims, letting them tell her where she needs to be and who she needs to kill. She should have been hunting the animals doing the killing.

She will start where she is. The vampires coming for her can come. She's ready for them. As long as they are looking for her, she will not have to search too hard. But she is also going to hunt them right back now. And when she is done, she will have done her bit to rid the world of some of the vermin. Arianna isn't moving purposelessly now. She is searching the woods for the dens where the dogs hide. It's not as easy for her in the forest as it is by the sea, and she strains for a whiff of them.

She finds a pack of three at last. They're asleep, but not for long. They pick up her scent before theirs makes it to her nose. She makes a mental note to bite into one of them so that that part of her awareness is enhanced. Already her stomach turns at the thought. But there is no time to entertain her nausea as she is surrounded by these dogs, not as big as the ones she saved Tanner from but nonetheless quite a size.

"Come to play, bitch?!" They growl, stroking their strange dicks.

"If this is a game to you, then let's play..." Arianna is composed in her resolve.

The three pull on their cocks so that soon enough they have full erections. They are serious about fucking her. They know that she is strong and would be able to handle it. Arianna despises their seriousness, the thought that she would actually want to fuck any of them. She spits onto the ground. The werewolves laugh. They stand so she can see their cocks. She's never thought to look before. But now she can't help it. Long, hairy dicks hang between their legs. Almost the entire shaft is covered in fur. She imagines that this must be a pretty uncomfortable fuck, even on purpose.

But that isn't all there is to these cocks. Just like other dogs, a deep pink, sometimes strangely blue head protrudes out as they arouse themselves further for her amusement. This colored bit extends quite a ways out of the furry part. She shakes her head...

"It might be better for you to put that shit away..." Arianna fills her tone with disgust.

They come down on all fours and immediately charge for her.

Arianna meets them head-on, not escaping into the air as her instinct normally has her do. The first wolf on her is a powerful beast and he knocks her to the ground, going for her with his teeth. He takes his head over her face, his vile breath consuming Arianna so that she feels she might pass out. She can't. She blocks the smell out of her mind and pushes so hard off the ground that both she and the wolf trying to bite her is in the air.

She holds him under his arms and turns over. Gravity does what it does and he is no longer trying to bite her, knowing that if she dies, or if he drops her, it's a long way down. Then Arianna bites into his shoulder hard and lets her teeth settle. Immediately her tongue is filled with fur and she wants to pull her fangs out. But she needs to register this hideous odor, this horrible flavor so that she can track werewolves easier from now on. Once she has what she needs she releases the bite, the wolf having bitten right back, also in her shoulder, and then shakes herself loose of the beast.

Then she is back on the others who are now trying to flee. She catches them quickly, their bulk making them clumsy and slow and so they tire quickly. Arianna makes quick work of them and soon they are both dead. She leaves them for the scavengers and goes off, hungry for her next kill but suddenly not feeling very steady.

She doesn't know that she has made two fatal errors. She allowed herself to be bitten by the wolf. And this beast she dropped from the sky, the one she bit, is not dead. As Arianna flies off in one direction, going deeper in the woods to look for more dens, this injured wolf crawls off to find his brothers. He knows that if they don't take Arianna down, she could start to make their lives very complicated.

By the time the injured wolf finds another pack, they've already heard of Arianna. The wolves are already in discussions with the Guard, sent to deal with this problem. They have made an unlikely alliance, knowing that if they work together it will be easier. Because of the scrolls that the Leadership has, they've discovered a secret about Arianna that not even Arianna knows. The vampire that bit her comes from a clan that cannot survive too long after they've gotten werewolf saliva in their bloodstream. This is her weakness. The wolves and vampires just have to wait it out now, tracking her until she is too weak to fight back.

The werewolves move through the forest with the vampires, collecting more and more wolves into the army. More vampires arrive too, Arianna sensing them all the more, her anxiety growing. She starts to think that she won't get out of England alive. She is okay with it if this happens. But she will take as many of the bastards to hell with her as she can. Suddenly she smells wolves and vampires everywhere. It's confusing and overwhelming. She knows that she is probably still adjusting inside to her new sensory skills. But she also knows that they seem determined to bring the war to her, and soon enough they will. For now, she needs to get some fresher air, and just as quickly as she was overcome with the smell of bats and dogs, it is gone. And Arianna now smells nothing, not even the stale smell of the city smoking just beyond the meadow.

At the edge of the forest, Arianna wonders at the way the forest opens into a meadow and then becomes a city. She looks over to where the meadow becomes countryside and cliffs and then the ocean. It seems an interesting coming together of times. It reminds her of her own meadow. She sits high in a tree, distracted by the changes happening in her body and trying to filter all the conversations in her ears that she isn't sure are happening in her head, or somewhere nearby. But then the giggles break into her head and she looks toward the forest floor.

Where the meadow meets the forest, seven young men, shepherds by the looks of it, have brought their maidens into the night for some fun. Arianna is bothered by the fact that she was already on top of them before she heard them. And the fact that, like the sudden silence in the forest, she now finds the world completely odorless, is really working on her.

Arianna watches them, close to each other, seven men, and seven women, probably not even twenty. They are all naked despite the weather, but their clothes are not too far from them. The men all have their staffs in hand as if these will be a match for the werewolves. But they need to feel like they've prepared themselves should they need to protect the women who have agreed to this risqué rendezvous.

Being the sucker for romance that she is, Arianna comes in a little closer, to watch as much as to be on hand in case of emergency. The nakedness in the grass is beautiful. All of them have the kinds of bodies that should be on paintings in museums or turned into sculptures. The moon shines down on them so that Arianna doesn't have any trouble seeing every detail of the scene playing out below her.

A dark-haired boy, the only one, seems a little shy as the woman he is with examines his penis. He seems almost ashamed of his erection. But the woman just runs her fingers along with his cock, and then she kisses him on his mouth. Arianna watches them, wanting to see what it is that has this young man so troubled. The woman encourages him to lie on his back. He doesn't want to but eventually does. Then Arianna gets it.

"It's okay...It's everything I want...You are everything that I want..." The woman has the most mesmerizing texture to her voice.

"But it's disgusting...You deserve so much better...You shouldn't have to deal with this..." He sounds bitter and angry when he looks at his dick.

This young man has a long scar across his crotch, starting on his left thigh and cutting diagonal all the way onto his chest. He's been attacked by wolves, a while ago probably, maybe even years ago. But he survived. His dick, erect, thick, and long, has a bend in it that is not natural. Arianna imagines that it was probably badly damaged during the fight. But it seems to have healed up well enough. It's a nice dick, thick and long just the way humans enjoy it. And the bend could be fun, Arianna imagines. The woman, who is now sucking it, seems to feel the same way.

Arianna watches as this boy's shyness disappears. He becomes more and more involved with the mouth on his dick and even the bend becomes his ally. He watches his cock being sucked with tender affection and makes plans in his own head to show as much tenderness. He pulls his woman to him so that her mouth stays on his dick but so that he can part her legs and look straight into her pussy.

After wetting his finger in his mouth he sends it into her. She wraps her cunt tight over the thick finger, sucking a little harder on the cock while her pussy gets to know the finger inside it. The acquaintance is made quickly and her cunt is moist enough for another finger. There is a slow insertion and then the dark-haired boy is fingering her with two of his fingers. She loves it, so he makes no additions, just watching his fingers slide in and out of her pussy while her mouth moves around on his cock. Soon enough they are side by side and he is easing the first part of his cock into her. A moment later all of him is inside her and they are making beautiful love.

There are two boys who look like they could be brothers. These two are cheeky, having the most fun with their women, it seems. They don't seem to have any issues with one another, having a conversation while their dicks are being sucked. They discuss the others around them, joking that they had all waited too long to start having sex with their maidens. But things have been a little tense. They compare dicks, and curse he who has the biggest cock.

The women seem to be easygoing too. They suck on these siblings and finger themselves. Then when the boys want to get in with their dicks, both women push their faces down to their cunts. They want to be taken care of with their tongues first. There'll be plenty of time for fucking later. They get down there, ever eager to put their mouths on these wet pussies.

Arianna watches these young people, losing themselves in one another despite all the shit that is going on around them. People are dying and there are demons everywhere. But still, they have found time and place to just be. The envy inside her meets the resolve she has to protect them. They are just all so fucking beautiful.

All the couples are fucking soon enough except one. In the end, furthest from the others is a woman who is sitting naked but hiding herself. The man with her is trying to convince her that it's okay if she doesn't want to. She keeps insisting that she wants to, but then holds herself closed so that he can't reach her relevant parts.

"It really isn't something that needs to happen now...it doesn't have to happen today..." The young man is really saying what his body is not proving, his erection at the ready despite his words.

"You're just saying that Luke, I know you don't mean it..." The young woman really looks like she is caught in the path of a wild beast that she can't escape, a beast that wants to consume her...

The man is patient. He kisses her softly all over her back and positions himself so that he hides her from the others. He runs his hand over her head and then lets his fingers move through her hair. He comes up close to her, opening his legs so that she is sitting between them. He speaks to her in her ear, lovingly, and then kisses the sides of her face from the back.

"I'm a virgin Luke..." she looks at him as though she expects him to take her home...

He comes around so he can look at her in her face. The more he tries to reassure her that it's okay, the more she is looking around at her friends who are making their men feel good. Luke hates that she is feeling inadequate and uncomfortable because of him.

"I know this...I know... We can go anytime you want. There will be other times when you are more ready...I've known for a while..." Luke looks at her and smiles with his eyes, amused that for almost a year now she has thought that she had him believe that she wasn't.

Arianna likes the way this woman calls her shepherd Luke. There is something about Luke that draws Arianna's focus to the two of them. She comes in a little closer, the moon high enough to do shit with her shadow. She moves through the trees quickly until she is close enough to see Luke clearly. She nearly falls out of the tree, remembering Tanner again. Luke looks exactly like Tanner, give or take a freckle. Arianna wonders if they are related. She wonders if things turned out okay for Tanner at the hospital.

Luke kisses his woman again. Then he slips his tongue into her mouth and moves on top of her. He does nothing but kisses her, not even letting his cock come into contact with her pussy. He just holds himself up over her, only her breasts rubbing against his chest because their lips are working together. Luke really takes his time.

Then he places just the tip of his finger on her clit, his mouth still on hers. Ever so gently he rubs the bean, letting it register this light touch. She opens her legs and then tries to close them. But Luke doesn't stop what he is doing but also doesn't stop her from moving however she wants. He just moves his fingertip over her clit until she is holding onto her knees, her legs wide. They are still kissing passionately.

Luke nudges against the entrance, gently. It is so delicious, just this place where her cunt folds from the left and right and covers her vagina. Luke slides his finger up and then down the length of the line that cuts her cunt in two. He makes no attempt to enter, just teasing her with the possibility of his finger.

When he is at the hole again she holds his finger there. Then she asks him in a whisper to try just a little. He does, easing the tip of his finger into her cunt. There is no rush. Luke makes small circles with his finger as he moves it through the entrance of his maiden's pussy. His cock beats as it contemplates how deep she might be, how tight, or if it will get to go into her.

Then he is fingering her easier. Arianna watches as this woman sets about letting Luke go into her with his finger. Luke never once goes at it too hard. He listens to her and lets her tell him what she wants. Arianna watches as Luke pulls his finger from her and then does the same thing to her cunt, with his tongue now. He is playing with his own cock while he eats out her pussy with his mouth, promising her that even this is enough for him.

The woman has her first orgasm. Luke is trying hard to bring himself there, knowing that if he cums then she will be relieved. But it is proving difficult despite all his reassurances to her. It will take a good while before he shoots from pulling on his own cock, having built himself up all day for pussy. He tries to beat his meat harder. But there is no sign of orgasm.

Still, he is sucking on pussy. He brings his woman to another orgasm. Then he moves up next to her so that her hands can reach his cock. He places her fingers on his balls. She plays with them while Luke pulls harder and harder on his own cock. The frustration of not being able to cum is showing on his face. He can't hide it. She takes the tip of Luke's dick and sucks hard. He asks her to go a little gently, he is already feeling tender. But he begs her to tug harder on his balls. She tries to give him everything he wants.

She goes into her cunt with her own fingers, trying to see her own limits. She manages to get three fingers into herself, but not completely. Just the first half of these fingers is in her, and she decides that she will just have to be strong. She really wants to give herself to Luke. She really wants tonight to be the night she loses her virginity.

She removes her fingers from herself but keeps her

mouth on Luke's dick. She plays with her clit while sucking him off so that her pussy is even wetter, another orgasm flooding and coating it. Then she is on her side, looking at Luke who really doesn't know what to do now as again his cock is left alone. He starts to play up and down his shaft and he wonders what is next.

His woman takes his hand off his cock and puts it between her legs. She helps his fingers into her. Then she urges him on top of her. She takes his dick between her legs and puts it on her cunt. Then she closes her eyes and asks Luke to be gentle, but to go in. He asks if she is sure. She is. He thanks his lucky stars and slides the first inch into her. He goes in another inch, slowly, trying to get a sense of where her virginity is.

When he gets to the tiny block she lets him know. He pulls out a little and just fucks the part of her vagina that he is already in. When she is ready, really ready, he goes into her until he pushes past her virginity and makes this woman his woman. She can't believe that he is inside her and that it isn't as bad as she thought it was going to be. Everyone had exaggerated the pain.

She is so excited that she wraps her legs around Luke so that he stays all the way inside her. She wants to feel him and draw from him the sounds that the other men are making. Luke still can't bring himself to fuck her harder. He just enjoys her, thanking her over and over for letting him in and for giving herself to him.

The seven men are now all inside pussy, and the women are caught up in the strength moving in and out between their thighs. Orgasms are plenty and the air is filled with the smell of these their copulation. Arianna wants to touch herself but it seems wrong to make herself a part of this perfection. She just lets them do their thing while she watches.

When they're getting dressed they talk for a little bit before the women need to leave. The shepherds are not allowed to be home before dawn, guarding the entrance from the forest until the sunrise being their jobs. There are no sheep anymore. Arianna watches as the females disappear into the meadow, the grass long. She remembers her own meadow but then shakes the memory from her head. The shepherds are still getting dressed, discussing their individual experiences as they cover up the dicks that have served them and their women well. Arianna is glad that she could have seen this.

Her head is suddenly yanked in the direction of the meadow, something in the air. Her eyes search for the women, seeing nothing. Where have they gone? Could they already be across it? It seems unlikely. Arianna tries to get her senses going, not sure what it is that is making her so unaware, still. She doesn't understand why she is feeling so unsettled, still. She obviously doesn't handle dogs very well. Nothing about her is working properly.

She goes over the meadow, trying to move along the path the women were running to get home before the morning milking. She doesn't see them. She looks up into the sky, but still nothing. They could not have simply disappeared. Then she hears it. A hissing that comes from far below, in the earth, through the long grass. Then she hears it all around her so that she isn't sure which way to go. All she hears is the hissing. There are vampires in the field, but where?

Arianna cannot, as hard as she tries, find where the young women are. She lands on the ground and pushes the grass out to the side as again she is walking the path of the maidens. There is just nothing here. Arianna realizes that she should probably have given herself a moment, a day, maybe more, to let her body make the adjustment. She is no good to anyone like this. She has no idea what is going on around her, and the hissing in her ears is driving her insane.

Then she hears grunts and growls, and she looks to where she left the shepherds. She goes toward the noise but arrives to find them gone. She goes up into the night sky to try to locate them but nothing. Then she sees it; flashes of movement on the forest floor. She goes down, following. The werewolves, a pack of about a dozen, have the seven in hand, held to them as they move as fast as they can through the woods.

There are screams that last just seconds somewhere in the meadow that Arianna has just come from. She doesn't look back, doesn't flinch. It won't help. She goes in the direction of the wolves; they will be easier to catch. She might save someone yet. But there is something about these wolves that is different. They move faster, in flashes, and then when they stop she has no idea where they are. This must be another clan, one she is yet to encounter in battle.

The wolves manage to elude Arianna and make it to their den, more a burrow than a cave. It goes down so deep that by the time they are in its bowels the humans can hardly breathe. It's moist and musty. They are all worried about their maidens but they know already that none of them made it home. And they all know that somehow it is their fault. They resign themselves to dying painfully in this darkness.

Their clothes are ripped off and the wolves move around them, lying naked on the soft earth. Thick tongues are licking them and they wait for the bites, the claws. But the wolves are just licking them, tasting. There is something uncomfortable, sinister in the way the wolves move their tongues over them, smell them, and lick the inside of their ass cheeks and then their balls. Then they hear one of the wolves saying that the vampires got the better deal and that the women would have been nicer. Another wolf reminds them that if they close their eyes it's all the same. And even if you don't close your eyes, ass can be pretty damn hot.

All seven realize what is going to happen to them. They swing their staffs until the wolves are bored and just pull them from their hands, throwing them to the floor. They know that there is no point in putting this off. Besides, all the wolves are fucking horny. And unfortunately, these particular beasts don't mind a little ass when pussy is scarce. All of the shepherds are in a total panic as their asses are spread wide, thick cold tongues slobbering their holes. Even with their panic, the sensation completely unfamiliar, the wetness of the fleshy tongues starts to send tingles through their dicks. The shepherds know that there is no hope of them being saved now since they too have no idea which way is out.

The dark is all around them, and they stop trying to see each other. They know that they won't see the light of day and so each of them says a silent goodbye to their friends. But then the wolves are no longer licking them, growling under their breaths. The burrow is so dark that they stop trying to see, grateful only that the cold wetness that was on their assholes is no longer there. The fact that it was turning them on was making them more awkward than if they had just been killed.

All seven get on the floor and feel around for their staff. When they can't find them, they just stay flat on the ground and cover their heads, not sure what is going on but understanding from the sounds the wolves are making and how they are circling that they are sensing danger.

The room fills with the sounds of a battle that nobody can see except those fighting it. There are thuds and snaps. Masses are thrown against the earth and then their necks are broken. Then there is dragging as the beasts are taken from the lair. The shepherds are going insane trying to figure out who this is. It can only be a rival pack. But they're sure they hear the sound of a woman. It can't be though. They just close their eyes unnecessarily and wait to see how this will end.

And then silence... then the darkness. The friends find each other and strategize a way out. They follow the breeze, a very slight wind. When it gets a little more intense they know that they are moving in the right direction. They hold on to each other and leave their staff. They search; looking for the light that will let them know which way is out. When they eventually step into the light they throw themselves into the sun, not caring that they are naked. Strewn on the ground are a dozen dead werewolves.

They go and stand next to the wolves to make sure that they are dead. When they turn back toward the hole they've just come from, they make out the outline of a young woman, with black hair and pale skin. The shepherds wonder why she moves so comfortably in the darkness and won't come out to them. Then they realize what she is. Arianna looks at them and then looks away, avoiding their nakedness, exhausted from the fight and anxious about the sunrise that threatens the horizon. She's seen their dicks before but they didn't know she was there. Now it's just awkward. Arianna can't help stealing glances at Luke through the corner of her eye, thinking of Tanner again...

When her eyes meet Luke's again she can see that he

has had nothing but vile experiences with vampires. Luke forgets very quickly that this woman has just saved him and his friends and he allows himself to be consumed by hate. The others are also already looking around for anything that they can use to kill this vampire. Arianna slips back into the hole, knowing that they won't follow her back down into the darkness that very nearly became their final resting place. As soon as night falls, she will get as far away from here as possible, so that she can let her body sort itself out... As she disappears into the earth, she can hear the shepherds screaming after her:

"We know what you are...We fucking know what you are..."

Arianna knows exactly what she is!

CHAPTER 5

TANNER SOON DISCOVERS that there is nothing more difficult to find than a vampire that doesn't want to be found. While everyone has stories, most of them are not true. And also, while people have probably never seen a vampire in real life, most of those that have never lived to tell the tale. Still, Tanner is persistent, even though, with the number of killings growing alarmingly, it is clear that there is not just one vampire in the area.

He travels through the villages trying to get as much information about Arianna as he can. He is careful not to mention that he thinks she is a vampire. He draws sympathy from the locals by tweaking the story, making Arianna his lover who he thinks has been taken captive by vampires, maybe werewolves. Everyone just looks at him as though he's lost his mind, but they try as best they can to get him the information he needs, or at least try and convince him to give it up. Who in their right mind believes that anyone taken by a vampire or werewolf lives longer than a few hours? These are animals. They're not in the habit of keeping pets.

The city is not yielding anything that might help Tanner, and he is starting to get the kind of looks that let him know that if he doesn't leave soon, or stop asking the kinds of questions he is, somebody might just commit him to an institution and promptly collect the fee that is paid for the handing over of lunatics. Of course, these lunatics are never seen or heard from again, ending up in top-secret scientific experiments.

The further Tanner moves into the country, the lighter he feels. It's too easy to feel like you're a part of the wallowing when one is continuously surrounded by self-pity or pigs. Also, he's heard about his brother and their run-in with the wolves. He's also heard the rumored twist that they were saved by a vampire. Actually, as Luke and his friends tell the story, Arianna attacked them just after they had defeated the wolves. And she too managed to send packing. Tanner knows the truth and so he needs to find his brother, to find out where they last saw Arianna.

But the shepherds also don't want to be found it seems. They've gone high up into the mountains, determined to build up the skill and strength they will need to exact their revenge. The truth is, they are more humiliated by what they know was almost going to happen to them. So their shame and anger and grief will be their motivation as they train each other to wipe out the wolves and vampires, armed with nothing but wit and shepherd's staffs.

The rain is making it all the more difficult for Tanner to move up and over the steep cliffs of the countryside. When he sees a rundown shack against the hill he is already sure he won't make it over today, he thinks that the gods are finally with him. It is the kind of structure that really hides itself well against the green and brown, but Tanner has a very sharp eye, despite his injuries acting up. Tanner staggers toward it, the gray sky getting darker as the rain falls harder. The cold is all the way through to his bones and the wetness is starting to soften his stitches, risking his wounds reopening.

By the time he gets to the shack, it is dark. He waits to see if there is a light that will come on to let him know that there is someone inside. As the night envelopes the country-side, the shack remains dark. Tanner gets up close and searches for a window. There isn't one. He peeps through the wider cracks in the rotting wood. Even with the rain falling hard he can hear movement inside. He wants to be inside.

Then there is an eerie silence. All movement ceases and Tanner tries to peep through the darkness. He can't make out anything. Suddenly the whole world goes a strange black that is darker than the night itself and Tanner loses consciousness. When he wakes up he is inside the shack, a modest mess, and two people are staring at him with suspicious, irritated eyes. The man is big, black, and hard working. His hands show the signs of a hunter. It was these hands that knocked him out. The woman looks out of place in this environment. Tanner wonders whose house she was stolen from. She's clearly had a pampered life but does a good job of pretending not to miss it.

"You'd better be quick about explaining what you're doing here sir..." The black man has the kind of voice that couldn't be aggressive for all his attempts.

It takes a whole lot of explaining and a whole lot of shivering before they start to believe Tanner. It does help that his scars can vouch for him. The couple introduces themselves, Catherine and Bartholomew. They look every bit like their names, in context. Catherine warms some stew, rich and meaty thanks to Bartholomew's skill in the woods, while they tell Tanner their story. It's as he had thought. Lady Catherine had fallen in love with Bartholomew, her fiancé's manservant. The love affair was discovered and this is the result, hiding, always moving, and never making fires for too long in case they are still being pursued.

Tanner appreciates the corner that they offer him, many skins available to warm him and also to keep him off the damp earth. The bed that Bartholomew shares with Catherine is itself layer upon layer of animal furs. It looks like it more than makes up for the fact that the fire that warmed Tanner's stew is already out, Bartholomew vigilant about protecting his woman, and their life. When they figure out how to get out of England, this is exactly what they plan to do. Tanner admires this love.

He tries to fall asleep as fast as he can, but it's hard. Tanner can hear that the pair who has been most generous with their tiny space is anxious about getting closer to warm up, but they are too polite to assume that their guest is sleeping. So they wait. Tanner waits for sleep to come, and Bartholomew listens for the sounds of sleep so that he can warm his woman. But it just isn't happening, and Tanner hates that he is the reason that these people who have been so nice to him are now feeling colder than they need to be because of him. So despite his claustrophobia, Tanner buries himself under the heavy furs and skins and hides himself so that the pair on the bed at least knows that he isn't watching.

Catherine is shaking loudly. There are moments, like this one, when she really can't pretend like it's as okay as she keeps telling Bartholomew they are. All he wants is for her to be in a beautiful comfortable home, warm enough for her to give him beautiful babies. He will make this happen. She knows that he will. In the meantime, he can keep her fed, safe, and warm. He can give her the only things he has; his body and his heart. Catherine is most content when Bartholomew makes love to her. He doesn't do it for himself. Everything about the way he makes love is about her. She loves him.

Bartholomew takes off his clothes and pulls his woman closer. He holds her against his erection and rubs it against her while taking her dress off. The wind outside beats against the wooden structure and there is an exaggerated sense of the cold. It really isn't as bad as it sounds. But that isn't to say that it isn't bad.

Even though Tanner is deep under his covers, he can hear every detail of what is going on less than a meter from him. The rain outside has become the kind of background sound that is largely negligible. Tanner can hear everything. It becomes louder and louder the more Bartholomew and Catherine try to make it quiet. Tanner can't help thinking that it would just be better if they could just pretend he wasn't here and fucked the way they are used to doing it. But he does appreciate their courtesy.

Bartholomew is careful not to throw Catherine's garments on the ground. He keeps them under the fur so that they are warm when he needs to put them back on her later. He pays so much attention to detail. This is why Catherine would rather be here with him like this, than anywhere else. He takes the time to do the little things that make even the worst big things not matter at all. Bartholomew is nothing like her father, mother, or brothers had led her to believe about Bartholomew's kind, as they had put it.

With his body close up against hers she starts to warm up. But the places inside her thighs that he wants to put his manhood inside are not ready yet. Bartholomew has to make sure she is incredibly wet before he even tries to insert his ridiculously large dick inside Catherine with her tiny pampered pussy. Fortunately, time is the one thing they have.

Bartholomew looks to where Tanner is under the remains of many of his hunts. If he could have sold these furs on the market he would be a very rich man. But this isn't possible. And looking at Tanner, remembering how cold and wet he was, Bartholomew is happy that he was able to offer his unexpected guest this little comfort.

Happy that he isn't able to see Tanner, Bartholomew will not keep Catherine waiting any longer. He goes under the fur and places his tender lips on Catherine's bare breasts. She holds his head, knowing that he is just starting what is going to be a very intimate night of fire-inducing passion. The hardness of Bartholomew's beard is down-played by the softness of his kisses on Catherine's breasts. She loves everything about the man she chose.

His mouth opens up over the entire breast that he is devouring. Bartholomew takes his time on each one. He isn't much of a talker during love-making, but without a word, Catherine knows exactly what he is saying. Bartholomew moves easily between her breasts and then onto her belly. She doesn't know how, but he seems to be touching every part of her at once.

When his mouth settles between her legs she cannot contain herself. She lets out a loud moan that soon sees Bartholomew's hand over her mouth. Because of how big he is, there is no need to move his mouth off of Catherine's pussy. She lets him hold her mouth shut, and wraps her legs around his head so that her cunt is given the same treatment from Bartholomew's mouth as her mouth is receiving from his hand.

His tongue settles completely over the surface area of her cunt. It's a large, flat tongue, thick and hot and strong. She loves the way it feels. He loves the way she tastes. Bartholomew's tongue moves in intense lapping movements over Catherine's pussy so that it warms up and stays warm even when Bartholomew moves off it to breathe. He is only off the pussy for a second at a time.

Then he covers her hole with his mouth and blows onto it. He is careful not to blow into her. What he does put inside her though is his tongue, and the combination of sensations has him hold a firmer hand over Catherine's mouth so that she isn't making as much noise as she is threatening to make. But he concedes defeat and just has to trust that Tanner is either sleeping or that he will understand, as a man.

Tanner is wide awake. He is more awake than he would be if he wasn't trying so hard to be asleep. So he uses the sounds coming from the bed to help him warm himself, believing that he too is out of sight, and also that the couple on the bed doesn't have the energy to focus on anything by themselves. All three adults in the room are now lost in their own worlds, Bartholomew and Catherine together, and Tanner feeding off them but alone.

Tanner moves his fingers up his cock, navigating the length of his tool. He hasn't really noticed how big his dick was until now, now that he is all alone under the covers with no one to pay attention to it but him. Tanner loves his cock. It's thick and long and perfect. There are no other fingers but his moving up and down his rod, the sounds from the bed giving him great pleasure. He is careful not to make any sounds of his own though as his masturbation intensifies.

Bartholomew is resting his tongue hard against the walls of Catherine's pussy. He is deep inside her and taking his time about enjoying her pussy. Catherine is happy that even now, in this cold wet weather, he is in no hurry to get inside her. She wants him there, but she also loves his tongue where it is, doing exactly what it's doing.

He gives her all she wants and then some. Then he is moving back up on her belly so that she has his mouth on her breasts again. As he does this he finds the entrance to her vagina and moves his finger tenderly into her. She has had several orgasms already, filling Bartholomew's mouth with her cum, and now taking his thick finger easily into her so that he too enjoys fingering her as much as she is enjoying being fingered.

Another orgasm has Catherine practically screaming. Bartholomew's head comes out of the warmth and into the cold room to check that Tanner isn't wondering what is going on. There is no movement that can be seen through the dark. The sound of the wind and the rain that are practically howling through the shack now means that one would have to be listening for the sounds of sex to actually hear them. Tanner is straining to hear everything while pretending not to be. His hand is under his pants, touching his dick directly, moving mostly in circles around the two or three inches closest to his balls so that he can pull on his nuts and touch at least some of his shaft at the same time.

Two fingers are moving into Catherine now. She knows that this is nothing like the cock waiting to get into her. She knows this very well. And she knows that she must enjoy this fingering for as long as she can because when Bartholomew is moving his dick into her cunt, she is going to have to be the one making concessions. It's such a huge mass of meat that she has no choice but to grit her teeth until her cunt acclimatizes. It always takes a while though, but she takes it, not wanting to make Bartholomew feel awkward about something he has absolutely no control over. Nature did this to him. Nature gave him almost thirty thick inches of dick. Fortunately, nature also gave him the heart to go with it...

It takes less than an hour for Bartholomew to give Catherine ten orgasms. Each one has her moaning sensually, feeding into the fires that Tanner is sending into his cock with his fingers. He isn't pulling hard on his dick. He is just stroking it gently so that when he eventually has an orgasm he is able to control it enough to simply exhale as he cums. He can't be heard, the embarrassment would be too much for him. Also, the idea of another man wanking to the sounds of his woman might piss Bartholomew off. And he's already knocked Tanner out once before.

Bartholomew has three fingers inside Catherine. He has them both covered now so that when he is kissing her, breathing is difficult but not impossible. The heat and smell under the covers are enough to lull them both into an altered state of consciousness. It's almost as if they are not sure what is real and what isn't. Bartholomew knows that this is the time to start feeding his donkey dick to Catherine. This is the perfect time for her to take it.

Bartholomew holds his cock as he places it inside Catherine. There is no urgency and he just feeds her his head. Catherine welcomes his cock inside her and lets her legs part a little more under the weight of her man. Bartholomew goes in a little more as she relaxes into his penetration. Thanks to his patience, it isn't long before all of his cock is inside her.

The filling sensation suddenly registers and Catherine has to calm herself without making Bartholomew uncomfortable. She wonders if their sex will always be like this, always consisting of this initial moment when she feels like she has too much dick inside her. There is nothing that can be done for the length that blesses Bartholomew between his legs. So she wills herself to enjoy it. She just needs to get through his first thrusts.

Bartholomew does his best to go slowly. But every single millimeter that he moves in or out of Catherine is overwhelming. His dick really is excessive. Still, he goes easy. He thrusts in small strokes, tiny movements in and out of her so that the bulk of his dick is inside her at all times. It takes a while, but soon enough Catherine is moving her tiny cunt around the dick as well, her pussy finally wet enough to come to the party.

Now their lovemaking can really begin. Tanner is trying to prolong his own pleasure as he registers the sounds from the bed. He doesn't want to cum too soon and then be left listening to them go at it for the rest of the night. But with Bartholomew now fucking Catherine incomplete, uninhibited thrusts, she is making the kinds of sounds that have Tanner really tugging on his thickness. He is going to blow at any moment.

Catherine spreads her legs even further apart. She tries to wrap them around Bartholomew but can't, he is just too broad. So she opens wide and lets him take care of business. He grinds down deep and then to the side. Bartholomew isn't trying to contain his own grunting now. Between Catherine's thighs is the fulfillment of all his dreams. And he isn't about to be apologetic about enjoying every bit of it.

They do seem to fuck forever. Tanner cums three times before he starts to drift off into sleep. He wakes a few times to find Bartholomew and Catherine still at it. He envies them both. Even when the sun has come up, or more precisely, the day has come, the rain and wind still beat against the resilient shack. Tanner makes no attempt to stir from under the furs until he is sure that the couple is awake and dressed. Then he comes up and joins them, embarrassed by the excessive stickiness in his own pants.

Bartholomew and Catherine don't let Tanner leave until he has eaten and bathed. Catherine manages a coat from one of the heavier furs as a gift that they insist he takes. The weather isn't playing games anymore, something almost dark and evil about the gray of the day, the heaviness of the clouds, and the persistence of the rain. Tanner thanks them, and continues on his search for Arianna, knowing that, as they wish him well on his quest, Bartholomew is already planning how to go about spending the day making love to Catherine the way he is used to...

Arianna has done a pretty decent job of leaving Tanner with a trail to follow. This wasn't intentional of course, and she was just doing what she had set out to do. But the trail of dead werewolves and vampires dotting the forest and countryside like breadcrumbs lets Tanner know that she was here. But the death doesn't last long, and soon enough Tanner runs out of bodies to follow. This is because Arianna herself is close to becoming a dead body too.

She can't keep up with the rapid pace at which the night becomes day and Arianna knows that she is going to need to find a place that she can rest up until this thing that has her ravaged by fever, goes away. The forest isn't really an option for her now because it is really quite full of vampires and werewolves that want her dead. And she hasn't the strength to fight.

Her best bet is one of the sheds on the farms that are close to the cliff's edge. She can be close to the sea while being able to see anything coming up on the hills. Also, it will be hard for the wolves and vampires to come at her in any real numbers in case the humans see them. Humans have taken up the fight with real gusto themselves now, figuring out mostly by trial and error how to kill both vampire and wolf. The miserable weather also means that the sun has become a little negligible during the long, wet, gray days...

Arianna finds her perfect hideaway. The shed is large and dark and well built. It hangs precariously over the edge of the cliff though and Arianna can't help but think that if the wind blew a little stronger, the whole thing would crash down into the sea. She reasons that if she is thinking like this, then others too would find it a little too precarious a spot to take refuge. So Arianna finds the darkest part of the shed and curls up to battle her fever, not knowing that the wolf she bit into left a little saliva in her when he fought back and that this tiny bit of spit is killing her.

Tanner doesn't even know that he's found her when he reaches the shed. He has pulled his coat so close to his face that he almost walked straight into the side of the structure. Arianna is delirious now and has no idea what is going on outside of her head. Her mind is filled with visions of Tanner, visions that even when she opens her eyes and sees him she thinks are not real.

"Arianna?!" Tanner has no idea how to approach her.

She looks wild and unpredictable, more like a rabid dog than the feisty warrior she was when she saved him from the wolves. He knows that it's her. Her face is the same. Her hair is as beautiful even now that it is wet with sweat and sticking to her face. The dress Arianna wears is tattered; giving testament to the journey she's traveled. Tanner doesn't know what is wrong with her. Neither does she. And even if she did, she would be unable to tell him. But still, he asks...

"What can I do to help you...what do you need?!"

Of course, Tanner knows that what Arianna really needs is coursing through his veins...and so he moves around her cautiously, knowing that if she did attack, she would not struggle to take from him what she wanted. He asks her the question a few times before accepting that she just isn't in a position to answer him.

He watches as Arianna rolls around on the floor. The rain has come into the shed, more from below than above. It's clear to Tanner that Arianna's body is in a battle to save itself. Tanner doesn't even realize that he's been watching her for almost a week, nibbling occasionally on the nuts and berries that he'd been gathering along the way, scavenged mostly from the dens of other scavengers, topped up with dried meat from Catherine. Arianna's fever seems to be breaking now and she is becoming a little more lucid. Now Tanner starts to worry about how she will respond to him being so close to her...

"Arianna..."

"Why are you here? ...You shouldn't be here..." Arianna still looks like she is in a lot of pain.

"I wanted to thank you...how can I help you?" Tanner is sincere...

"You... Help me... How could you possibly help me?" She writhes on the floor, dripping massive amounts of sweat and shaking uncontrollably for a while so that she cannot speak until the shaking ceases.

"Arianna this is no time to be proud. What do you need me to do for you?" Persistence is clearly one of his strongest qualities.

There is no way for Arianna to respond now because again she has passed out, her fever animating her so that Tanner is sure that she is going to die at any minute. He looks through the slit under the door at the far end of the shed. The rain is coming down so incredibly hard that the sight of a couple of dogs trying to get in is both inconsistent and also somewhat expected.

The dogs claw at the door for two days. This is something that gets Tanner very anxious. The dogs don't seem to want to get at them. They seem anxious to get away from something that they sense is coming on the outside. Tanner knows that it is a good idea for them to get going.

"We're going to need to move Arianna. We need to find somewhere else..." Tanner speaks as though he knows what Arianna's plans were. He speaks almost as if he knows that a pack of wolves has picked up on Arianna's scent and that they are just beyond the farm at the bottom of the hill.

"We need to move Arianna...Something is not right..." Tanner becomes all the more urgent. Arianna is unable to respond still, moving in and out of consciousness. Tanner knows that she probably needs to eat. He can only imagine how long it's been. Tanner needs to get some blood into her. He holds his hand against her mouth, then his neck. Arianna turns away.

"Not you...not you!" Arianna manages to speak at last.

"Come on Arianna just a little bit, so you can get your strength up. We need to move. And it's not pretty outside..." Tanner doesn't even know for sure what it will mean for him to give his blood to her.

"Not you!!!" she almost yells. Tanner knows it's pointless.

From the way she is breathing in his scent, particularly where he has blood that has clotted on the surface of his skin, Tanner knows that she needs blood. He wishes that she would just take his. But she won't. And when he thinks of all the stories he heard about Arianna on his searches, the stories he heard about the killings that involved a vampire woman, he remembers something that stuck out for him, something that made him fall all the more in love with her and want to find her all the more...

He remembers that she only ever killed really bad men!

The wolves are close now, her dying body sending out her location. Tanner doesn't want to leave her but he knows that he needs to find her a meal. The farm they are on doesn't seem to have a lot of staff, if any at all. There might be a family in the farmhouse. But they might just be good people. There might be animals in the other sheds too. But he doesn't know if their blood will do. Tanner knows one thing for sure, thanks to his instincts. He knows that whatever is coming for Arianna, and now him, must be very close indeed...

Tanner runs through the door and makes sure that it is closed behind Arianna to protect her from the dogs. Then he runs toward the farmhouse, the only building with a light on. The closer he gets he sees that the light is from a candle in the kitchen. But there is nobody in the room. He goes closer, the dogs at his hills, hysterical but not charging for him as such.

Then a woman comes into the kitchen, followed by another one. They look like sisters. And both of them are beautiful despite the obvious hardness of their lives.

"You go first today Grace, please. I'll start supper." The woman is already stoking the fire on the stove.

"Okay, Anne...He's had quite a bit of ale, so maybe he won't last too long..." They both laugh. Grace doesn't mind taking one for her sister. They've just started with the potatoes and a growling sound comes from somewhere in the old house. The voice calling for Grace sounds like it belongs to a very old, very drunk man.

Tanner watches to see which direction Grace goes and

then follows her. He gets to the window of the bedroom, a large man lying on the bed playing with his cock. "Come and please your husband... I make you happy don't I Gracie...You and Anne...Who else would have taken on the responsibility of two women...You are happy out here with me right?" He speaks as though he knows that his words carry no weight with the women but he wishes they did. Tanner has seen this story so many times, young women from poor families are sold off to old men with two pennies to rub together.

Grace gets naked and then on the bed with her husband, a husband she shares with her younger sister. He lifts her skirt and scolds her jokingly for still having her knickers on. She starts to take them off but moves too slowly for him so that he pulls them down off her and throws them on the floor. Then he pulls her dress up over her head and throws this too on the floor. His hands move hard against the woman's firm little body.

He takes her breasts into her mouth and moves his hand between her legs. Grace is already rubbing his cock, making it firmer with her fingers. His fingers are inside her. He has put more than one into the tight cunt so that Grace is moaning already. Her husband puts his mouth on hers to keep her a little quiet as he rolls on top of her. Every time Grace sounds uncomfortable then Anne has a tough time taking his cock into her.

With a semi-erection, he moves into Grace and starts to thrust. The old man must be hard completely now because he is really making her moan deeply. His mouth is on hers in vain because each thrust makes her pull her mouth to the side and ask him to slow down until she's ready. He just tells her that he loves her and keeps going. This gives Tanner an idea...

He goes to the kitchen and watches Anne through the window for a while. Then he takes a big risk and taps lightly on the window. She looks to where the sound is coming from and then looks back at her pots, convinced that it's just the rain. Again Tanner taps, and this time when she looks at the window, the lightning reveals the man in the window. He has a finger on his lips, begging her not to scream. Anne and Grace see few people so the excitement of another person has Anne open the window slightly while ensuring that the door is bolted.

"I need your help!" Tanner is desperate.

"What? Where are you from? Who are you? Why are you here?" Anne is throwing questions at him in anxious whispers.

"My friend is very sick, and we need to get moving. But I need something that only you can give me..." Tanner is having trouble making his request so that he isn't scaring Anne.

"What could possibly have to give you?" Anne has a naïve curiosity.

"I need a little bit of your husband's blood?!" Tanner says it after a long pause.

"What? How will that help you and your friend?" Anne is now really nervous.

"I don't have the time to explain. But if you can just cut him, just a little, and let some of the blood collected on the sheet, I'll just take the sheet and be on my way..." Tanner speaks so casually that even Anne suddenly thinks this is the most normal thing in the world...

"It takes a while for me to receive him, and even then I'm usually so uncomfortable that he finishes before I can even think of my own pleasure..." The practical answer has Tanner taken aback.

"I can get you ready for him if you want. I need you..." Tanner will prepare her pussy if that's what it takes. It's going to take quite a bit from him, and he is going to need to make his own massive dick really work on the woman who has already admitted to having difficulty receiving her own husband.

Anne doesn't know what she is doing or why, but she unbolts the door. She knows that her husband won't come out of the room until she has gone in. And she knows that it will be a while before he is satisfied with Grace. Tanner is taken over by the warmth from the stove and he remembers Arianna. He mustn't indulge. He needs to make this quick.

He stands near the stove until he is sufficiently dry. Then he pulls Anne into the pantry and gets on his knees, lifting her skirt over his head. He pulls down her panties and kisses her hairy pussy. He searches for her clit and finds it eventually. Then he licks it gently. He searches for her hole and goes into it. Anne has never had such pleasure.

She pushes him off her and asks to just see his dick. She's only ever seen her husband's. Tanner obliges, but he doesn't want to waste time. Anne takes hold of Tanner's cock and puts it in her mouth. She's not had much experience sucking a dick but Tanner tolerates her enthusiasm. His erection excites her even more. Anne pulls Tanner to his feet and asks for just a little bit inside her. He has no choice. He needs her to help him.

Anne cannot believe the pleasure she feels as Tanner's cock slides into her. Tanner goes about half in and starts to thrust in circles so that her pussy gets wet quickly. He needs the old man not to struggle today. Anne holds on to him so tightly, thanking him, and begging him to kiss her. She just wants one kiss. Tanner again obliges, hoping that Grace will appear and call for her any second. He needs Grace to call her before she cums or this plan will backfire. They hear Anne's name just in time...

"If you hurry now your husband will get you to the end. You will enjoy him today, I promise...Don't forget me now. I really need your help." Tanner pushes her out before Grace comes in. He makes sure that she has the blade needed.

While Grace goes into another room to change Tanner hurries out of the house and around to the window where he can see if Anne will come through for him and Arianna. He is pleased to see the young woman riding her husband's dick, much to his delight.

"I must always make you wait...It makes you enthusiastic. You love me don't you?" He makes the whole thing about him. In Anne's head, it is all about Tanner. Then she drops the blade in the sheets and plays with her tits so that her husband can keep his focus on her. He fucks her from below and she rides him from above. Tanner crosses his fingers.

Then the old man starts to wriggle under her, looking confused. She asks him what's wrong and he just lifts her off his dick. Then he sits up and Anne can see the red on the sheet behind him. She says nothing for a minute just so that there is a little more blood before she screams and Grace comes running into the room.

"Dammit...I must not have put the blade away properly..." He blames himself, apologizes to her, and looks for what cut him. "I'm just glad that it didn't hurt you, my love..." He really does care for his wives.

Grace deals with the wound while Anne gathers the sheets and leaves the room. Tanner is already at the kitchen door to receive them. He thanks her and hurries to where he left Arianna. He hopes it isn't too late.

But by the time Tanner gets back with the blood, it is

too late. Arianna is nowhere to be seen. There's a smell in the shed that Tanner knows from previous experience. He looks around wildly, panic filling him. Then he sees them. Two large wolves step out into the space and gnarl. Tanner just drops the blood-soaked sheets and then falls to his knees, too tired to even try and fight.

"Oh no, human...your death won't come that easy...we have a show planned for you that you will never ever forget..." One of the wolves speaks directly into Tanner's face before knocking him unconscious and throwing him over his shoulder. They move to catch up with the others...

CHAPTER 6

THE RAIN IS REALLY COMING DOWN NOW and the hills are difficult to negotiate. But the werewolves are in high spirits. They have what they've been looking for. This was easier than they thought it would be. Arianna proved herself to be a less than challenging adversary after all. And now she is weak and vulnerable, not as appealing. This isn't to say that they won't enjoy her though.

The vampires will be here in a few days, once they've received the news. The messenger has been told not to treat the message as urgent, and to take his time about delivering it. But before he leaves, he gets to take the first dip in Arianna's pond.

"Remember me?" the dog snarls as he rubs his face against hers, pointing to where she bit him. "You really shouldn't have dropped me..."

He tries to sound even more threatening than he looks. Arianna just turns her face away. There is something about his smell that makes her want to throw up. It just seems to really get into the parts of her that are making her sick. This is because it is this very wolf who made her sick.

As she turns she is staring directly at Tanner. They have him tied to a stake, naked. The wolves are slowly reopening all the wounds that had already started to heal. She locks eyes with his, worried more about what they are doing to him than with what she knows is going to be done to her. She can handle these beasts.

"You shouldn't have come for me..." Arianna manages just this sentence. She closes her eyes, respecting Tanner enough not to see his nakedness. But he is beautiful to look at. And that his new wounds are because of something he feels for her makes her warm inside. Tanner can't close his eyes as the wolf standing over Arianna takes all she has on off.

The dog gets on her and sends its tongue into her mouth. She can't bring herself to bite it, knowing suddenly somehow that this spit that is filling her mouth is a problem in her bloodstream. Then his tongue is on her neck, her breasts. A moment later he is licking her cunt hard, sending his tongue all the way inside her. Arianna is surprised by how the cold doesn't make her shiver. She doesn't even flinch.

The werewolf's tongue really fills Arianna's cunt. It goes so far into her that she feels the slippery sensations in her belly. She refuses to look down, not wanting to see the effect this tongue is having on her pussy, which seems to be responding favorably to the movements inside her. She feels her clit tingle, then her thighs. She remembers how they showed off their dicks when she mocked them and told them to put them away. If there is one thing that is clear, it's that this particular wolf, bearing scars from a close encounter with Arianna, is really going to enjoy being the first wolf inside her vamp-vagina.

He pulls his tongue from her and then runs a claw

lightly over her pussy. Still, she is not looking to where he is busy on her pussy, the others walking around them, some helping part her legs, also licking the available parts of her. Arianna doesn't resist. She doesn't fight, understanding the logistics of war and its spoils. The wolves mock her as her clit blooms and it is clear that her body wants what her head might not have imagined it ever would.

Because of their size, they build the altar-like bed a little higher. It's hard, made of rocks and stumps and mud. Arianna expected nothing more. So when her back is pierced by the materials used to build this fuck nest she just breathes deep and lets her full weight settle on the hardness. The sooner she accepts it the better. She knows that there is nothing that she can do about it. So she doesn't even try. Again she is looking to where they have placed Tanner.

"I'm sorry..." Tanner mouths.

Arianna just looks away, knowing that there is nothing that she can say to let him know that this is not his fault. And that in fact, she is the one who should be sorry for him.

Suddenly a hairy thickness fills Arianna and she closes her eyes. The wolf is moving into her pussy with a little part of his paw. The beast is warned not to shred her cunt because there is quite a queue of dick wanting to get in there. And the vampires will probably also want to have fun with her when they arrive. So the wolf pulls out and shows his mates that he has retracted his sharp, jagged claw. Arianna's cunt is wet and so the paw is dripping in cunt juice and sweat when it is pulled from her.

Arianna hates that Tanner will these animals fucking her. She knows that she won't be able to hide her body's response from all those watching. She hates that even if they made it out of her now, Tanner would probably want nothing to do with a woman who was fucked by the werewolves that killed so many people that he loved. But her body is weak. She hasn't fed in a while. So she has no way of controlling her pussy so that she appears to be offering resistance. And the unusual combinations of cold, hairy, and slimy make her very horny. She puts it down to her fever.

Tanner watches as Arianna is licked by every wolf within reach. Every time he tries to look away he receives a slow clawing across his face so that he opens his eyes or risks having his face torn off. He doesn't want to meet Arianna's eyes. Tanner doesn't want her to see the lie they will tell her, the lie that will have her think that he thinks that he can save her. Because now, as they torture him, making him watch as the wolves start to prepare their cocks to fuck the woman he loves, they both know that nothing can save them now. He can also sense that her body is more than just a little involved in what is going on to her.

He watches as Arianna has her legs held far apart. The wolf is already dropping long, stringy strands of saliva on his cock. It's a hideous-looking cock, strangely shaped and oddly colored. Then there's the fur. Tanner isn't sure if he should feel sorrier now for Arianna than he knows he would have if he was watching her being fucked by a normal dick. There is nothing normal about the cock that is now being used to beat down on Arianna's pussy as though he were trying to knead it into submission.

The thick tip, bluish-black, moves into Arianna while his buddies hold her legs. They watch as the slimy first half of the cock moves up into Arianna and fills her so that they can see the tip of this dick create a dome on her belly. He has gone in and then up, not down as one would expect a cock to do. But then again, dogs aren't designed to fuck like humans. So he has Arianna in the incorrect position. But this doesn't bother him, or matter to the others. This fucking isn't for her comfort. But they are determined to make it pleasurable, punishing both her and Tanner.

Arianna is taking short and shallow breaths as the wolf starts pumping hard into her pussy. The others whistle, bark and grunt loudly. Then they all start to howl in unison. The wolf inside Arianna is lost in his own world. He finally understands what the hype is around the power of a vampire cunt. The muscles inside Arianna seem to have a mind of their own and it feels like she is fucking him right back and giving him a hand job all at the same time. The wolf fucks harder, howls louder, and tells the others what exactly it is they're in for. They can't wait now.

Even when dog dick is placed in her mouth Arianna doesn't flinch. The taste doesn't even bother her because it is no worse than the smell. What does get to her is the constant rubbing of hard, tangled fur against her skin. It reminds her of things she doesn't know. But whatever that memory is that is gnawing at her, revived by this sensory assault, she is almost convinced that this is worse than anything else. But the cock moving in her pussy makes all the bad textures and sensations negligible.

Then her legs are lifted high as the wolf inside her fucks harder. Two dicks are in her mouth now, dripping with sour-smelling semen. She is ordered to swallow. She doesn't. They drop more semen into her mouth and hold her mouth closed with their dicks until she swallows, needing to open her airway so that she can breathe. They keep filling her with semen, forcing her to drink it. The wolf in her cunt is going harder and harder now, wanting to fill her with his own seed as well.

He pumps wildly now as he watches his mates fill her mouth to overflow. There is the smallest of sounds coming from Arianna, involuntarily. But still, her moans make the confirmation needed for them to know that she is unable to fight her body's response to their fucking. She's obviously not been fucked in a while, not by the kind of power that her body needs for it to be satisfied. The wolves are impressed with her strength.

Eventually, there is slippery coldness inside her and she knows that the wolf has cum. She dismisses it quickly, knowing that the next one is already getting into position as the messenger is now free to go and summon the vampires and tell all the wolves he runs into that they have some delicious cunt if they want to hurry to the secret location and get a taste before the vampires arrive to fetch her for themselves.

The wolves become wilder and wilder the longer they have to wait. It's the visuals. Watching dick move in and out of Arianna's snug snatch is quite a sight. Also that they can see the cock move around inside her makes them happy, knowing that they are really giving her cunt a solid beating that it can take, beating the dick right back. Tanner bows his head and takes as much clawing into his face as he can before he has to look up again. He is happy though that Arianna is obviously not in any pain.

She takes every dick and swallows every load that is dropped into her mouth. When they move their dicks too far down her throat she takes it, knowing that they can't kill her by suffocating her. So she just takes their punishment without making her punishers too proud that they're doing anything extraordinary. But this in no way means that she doesn't feel everything that is being done to her. She just refuses to show it. But she knows that she won't be able to hide her orgasm, which is coming over the horizon.

Tanner cannot take it, either way. Watching Arianna being fucked hurts him. The claws on his face, digging into his skin, hurt him. The claws that have now reopened all his wounds hurt him. This is the kind of stuff that nightmares are made of. Tanner has just had all his nightmares handed to him on a silver platter, courtesy of these smelly dogs. It was not what he had expected when he started his search for Arianna. But one thing is for sure, he has now found her.

Arianna doesn't give them the satisfaction of screaming. She doesn't need to. The moans on each thrust are enough for them. She hates what this means to Tanner, so she goes to a place in her head that she didn't think she would have the strength to. She finds the shed again, the one where Tanner found her, the one where he held her for days until she was feeling better. Arianna manages to get there in her head, alone with Tanner, and both of them are in a better physical condition than either of them has been in weeks. She might not be able to control who is giving her her pleasure. But she will not let the same be true in her head.

Arianna closes her eyes after giving Tanner one more look, absorbing his nakedness now, and loses herself in a waking dream, creating every detail as she wants it so that the reality has no effect on her...

Despite the rain, the shed is dry. It's also warm, a fire in the earth that Tanner must have started. It doesn't matter. There is a fire and Arianna is warm. Tanner is already on the ground, reclining on a large skin. He is calling her to him. His nakedness glows beautifully in the light of the fire. There is something supernatural about how this makes him glow. It is not what Arianna expects, even in her own imagination. But it really is important that she makes him stronger in her dream than he has managed to be in real life.

Arianna gets on the animal skin next to Tanner and closes her eyes as he removes her clothing. Naked, she opens her eyes to find Tanner looking her up and down. Then he comes in and kisses her, raising Arianna's core temperature more than it's been in her entire afterlife. Tanner wraps himself completely around Arianna and fills her mouth with the softness of his tongue. He tastes like things Arianna remembers from childhood, before the turning. His tongue in her mouth is not uncomfortable. It is in fact very comforting. She cannot imagine another tongue in her mouth.

"You are everything that I have ever wanted" Tanner whispers when he removes his tongue from her mouth. Arianna kisses her response.

The feeling of Tanner's cock against the inside of her thighs makes her feel even warmer. Arianna wraps her legs around Tanner's now and he pulls her even closer to him, her breasts gently pressed into his chest. It feels like they could just stay like this forever. Arianna is where she wants to be, with who she wants to be therewith. Nothing else is needed now.

When their mouths separate again Tanner immediately places his lips on Arianna's neck. His teeth and tongue make contact with the delicate flesh there as well. Tiny tremors move quickly over the surface of Arianna's skin and she feels like she might take flight. Inside her head, there are millions of bubbles, and her belly is filled with millions of butterflies. This is a feeling she has never felt before.

"Is this love Tanner..." She asks as he continues on her neck...

"This is everything, Arianna..." He ends the verbal conversation...

Tanner's fingers move down her belly and onto her clit. There are more butterflies. He traces the shape of her sensitive clitoris along the edges of the pink organ and then gives it a few gentle taps with the tip of his finger. Then his finger slips between the slit and finds her hole. Tanner's finger is *thick and strong and as he tentatively moves around the entrance to Arianna's cunt he sends a thousand unfamiliar sensations through her body.*

Then more of his finger is inside her. Arianna parts her legs so that Tanner can do what he is doing with ease. He lets her fall onto her back and then rubs the inside of her thighs while he continues fingering her with just one finger. He watches as her pussy receives him over and over again, getting more and more wet. Tanner will be inside her soon. Arianna knows that it won't be long before he gets into her because this is her dream and she will make it so.

Tanner replaces the finger on Arianna's cunt with his mouth. And then his tongue is inside her. She holds his head firmly and moves her pussy in tiny circles so that Tanner works through it completely with his tongue. Tanner fills her so that the warmth moves through every part of her body. The fire even feels unnecessary. But it doesn't make it any less welcome.

Then Tanner is off her pussy with his mouth and back in her with his finger. There is a brief moment where he lets her enjoy his single finger before sending another one into her. Then he adds another one. And Arianna is caught in an absolute euphoria that has her wetter than she has been in her entire life. So she takes all his fingers that he wants inside her. And her pussy is wet in anticipation for the cock that she knows is coming.

When Tanner comes back up onto her mouth with his lips Arianna is again in heaven. There is contentment in his mouth that makes Arianna believe that there is nothing else in the world that he wants. She knows as he kisses her now that she is all he wants. Even that she has created this in her own imagination doesn't take away from the fact that she feels that she too, as he, is all that Tanner wants.

Then she feels his cock against her pussy. He rubs it all the way up and down her slit and then massages her clit with the tip of his cock. She cannot be any wetter inside. Her body aches for him and he knows it. Finally, Tanner moves his dick into position and starts to slide it into Arianna. She exhales as she receives all of his meat. It is every bit as strong and able as she needs it to be. It is as much a contender for her satisfaction as any vampire cock. But this is cock she wants. It isn't dick that she is force-fed by arrogance.

Tanner and Arianna melt into each other as he begins his lovemaking. It feels for Arianna that Tanner is infusing her with the warmth from the fire. Each thrust fills her with incredible bursts of satisfaction. The power in Tanner is incredible. There is nothing weak or inadequate about his strokes. Arianna has no doubt that she is going to be completely satisfied.

Her pussy is expanding all the way to the back, deep inside herself as Tanner moves his dick to its furthest reaches. It stretches wide as his cock thickens ever more on each thrust. With Tanner's dick as big as it's going to get, Arianna settles her pussy around it and again they are moving into each other. This is exactly how Arianna thought lovemaking would feel. Creating it herself is working out very well for her. She has forgotten all places except this one that she has created in her head for herself and her lover.

Then Tanner moves his cock from inside Arianna so slowly that she has another orgasm by the time he has withdrawn completely. His mouth is on her cunt again as he lifts her legs over his shoulders and eats out her wet cunt. More orgasms follow as Tanner uses his tongue, lips, and then fingers on Arianna before turning her onto her tummy, raising her at the hips, and digging back into her cunt from this new position. He fucks her in beautiful scooping strokes.

His hands go all the way underneath her body with his dick all the way inside it. He touches her breasts tenderly and then not. Tanner responds perfectly to the desires of Arianna's body, never missing a scoop, lifting her over and over off the warm fur using nothing but his dick. Arianna herself doesn't need to do anything but enjoy it. Her pussy is squeezing and gripping and hugging and tugging on every inch of Tanner's cock that is now scooping her cunt in exaggerated sweeps.

After bringing her to yet another orgasm, Tanner has them on their sides. He holds Arianna close to him and gives her his cock in long slow strokes, with her eyes on the place between her legs that his dick is moving through. It is the most beautiful thing she has ever seen, this large, loving penis, solid in its effort to make every part of her wet. He lifts her leg over his and kisses her back. He bites into the back of her neck and then kisses the side of her face. He pulls her legs further back over himself so that they can both watch his cock at work.

It isn't long before Arianna is on top of Tanner, his cock still inside her. He moves her around on top of him while continuing his movements inside of her. Tanner is almost as precise with pleasing Arianna's pussy as Arianna has been about killing. Arianna is putty in his hands as she completely surrenders herself, body and mind, to Tanner in her head. He too is completely hers in this love nest.

On her stomach again, Tanner is still going at her cunt with determined thrusts. She has stopped counting her orgasms. His dick never leaves her pussy, moving around inside her so creatively that she feels almost inadequate and undeserving. This is everything that she wants. She hopes that she is satisfying enough for Tanner as well. He tells her over and over that she is. He assures her that she has nothing *to worry about. And then he resumes his intense lovemaking...*

But the reality is very different. The wolves are taking every care to take their dicks on a very scenic tour of Arianna's cunt. Fortunately for Arianna, this isn't where she is. In her head, she is somewhere else with Tanner. But the wolves are savoring every aspect of her pussy. They enjoy watching each other on her almost as much as they enjoy it when it is their turn. They enjoy watching her pussy secret evidence of the pleasure they are pumping into it.

The turns come quick and fast. A particularly mangy beast is now between her legs. For animals that don't take kindly to water, these creatures are just constantly wet. One thing that these wolves are enthusiastic about is fucking. They don't even care that it's Arianna anymore. It's all about having a pussy that can take dick after dick until each of them is satisfied.

With her pussy wet from semen and her own flow, something that she is producing because of the power of her imagination, the large cock moves into her all the way. The others are again excited as first the uncovered half, then the furry base of the cock goes into Arianna. They hold her legs wide so that everyone who wants to see can see. They position her so that Tanner too can see clearly every aspect of the fucking. They pull on his cock, willing him to have an erection, promising him that he can get some if he can just get hard. They rub their erections against Tanner, teaching him about what an erection is as though he has no idea. Tanner closes his eyes as his body tenses, knowing that these wolves are capable of anything.

The wolves taunt Tanner aggressively, licking him, placing the tips of their cocks against him, and then close to his ass, rubbing their hairy shafts between his cheeks.

Tanner's instinctive response amuses the wolves. But despite his body's resistance, Tanner challenges them to take him instead, to do what they want with him, but to please let Arianna go. The wolves promise Tanner that they can get to him too if it's what he wants, but that they know as does he that he doesn't have the same strength that the immortal has, so he won't be as much fun for as long. They make it clear to Tanner that there is still a way to go on Arianna, more wolves on the way, and of course, the vampires.

Tanner can't take it anymore. He begs to die. He screams over and over for them to kill him. They laugh at him, assuring him that death will come, but not yet. His face is held so that he has no choice but to look directly at Arianna. She has been turned to him and her legs parted so that Tanner can see into her cunt. The wolves part it a little more and then send fingers into it. Tanner tries to look away and is clawed at his side until he looks. His screams have brought Arianna out of her happy place and the reality hits her hard, almost as hard as the thrusting now going on between her legs. Again she faces the truth of who and what is really wetting her cunt.

He watches as they hold her up so that another wolf sits underneath her. Then she is lowered so that this dog can have her riding his cock. The wolf holds her hard onto his dick that has gone all the way up her tattered cunt. He moves her violently around on his dick and she bobs around on him like a ragdoll. Arianna's fever has her shifting into semi-consciousness. The fates have proven very cruel not just to her, but to Tanner, who just couldn't leave well enough alone, but had to try and help those who couldn't help themselves.

Three wolves have Arianna sit on their dicks like this.

The last one forces himself into her ass when her vagina is too slow draining itself of the slime that has filled it excessively. It takes most of his strength to force his dick into Arianna's tight behind but he insists on getting in there, edged on by the others. When he is done with her she is not even able to open her eyes at will. Her body is finally starting to fade again, her thirst too much for her now, and the werewolves' dicks proving beyond her current capabilities. It's starting to feel like a dream.

Tanner and Arianna start to anticipate their deaths. There is no way out of this mess they find themselves in. But both of them are soaked in cold water, the wolves throwing bucket after bucket over them to revive them. There is a commotion outside and all the wolves look at Arianna at once, one of them slapping her a bit so that eventually her eyes open. With a grin so evil that it is matched only by his sinister growl, the wolf who is fucking her tells her that the party has just begun...

CHAPTER 7

IT ISN'T TOO long before the vampires arrive. There are just three, but both Arianna and Tanner know that in their current states, even one would be enough to end their lives. Ending their lives isn't high on the agenda though, clearly. The three ignore Arianna and go straight to Tanner first, inhaling the places where blood oozes from him. They give him a long licking before sucking a little bit from his wounds, nothing too hectic. All Tanner can do is pretend it doesn't hurt. But he isn't very good at pretending.

Arianna watches Tanner for a minute while the wolf on her finishes up. He is the last one. And he has left her pussy wet and throbbing. She can't place what exactly it is about the way the dogs fuck that has turned her cunt inside out like this, what it is that has made her so unexpectedly wet to the point that she at times couldn't hide her ecstasy. The wolf pulls out and then gives her pussy a few licks while Arianna tries to orientate herself.

She sees the three vampires a little more clearly now. There are others too, twelve, humans. Arianna knows them but she can't say immediately from where. Then unexpectedly another wolf is on her. Tanner yells out and the vampires take in this obvious connection between vampire and human. They wonder if Arianna feels the same way about him. But she isn't giving anything up, her pussy already a rhythmic erotic mess as the wolf fills her with himself and brings her to an orgasm.

Then the vampires are around Arianna, taking in the smells coming up from between her legs. It's already got their dicks hard. But they are not in too much of a hurry. Besides, they've brought some additional entertainment. They call the humans, dirty-looking savages so that they can come and have a look at her pussy. The humans are told to smell it and lick it. They do. Then one of them sticks an enthusiastic finger in it. He fingers Arianna until she starts to respond. This excites the human and he goes harder and harder until she has a very loud orgasm. The other humans pat him on his back.

"We've brought you some friends, Arianna..." The voice is familiar but Arianna doesn't care too much to look.

Her fever has her caught in an almost continuous flux now, where she isn't sure what is and isn't real. What she does know however is that everything that is playing out between her legs is fantastic. She doesn't look to see who is playing. She can't even raise her head. All she knows is that she has an insatiable desire to be fucked continuously now, her clit rattling and her pussy aching deep inside each time it is touched.

"She really seems to be enjoying herself..." The vampires look at Tanner, making a statement and asking a question all at the same time.

"Fuck you all..." Tanner is finished.

The three who've now completely taken over the show watch as Tanner tries to turn away from the pleasure

Arianna is about to be given by these vile-looking savages. There is no time to process the parts of him that wish it was him. All he can manage is the parts of him that wish it wasn't them, here, now. He can only wish it wasn't like this.

The humans are naked now. They are possessed of the kind of dicks that have them stroking their own meat proudly so that the wolves and the vampires look. As far as humans go, the dicks are all impressive. Tanner's is as impressive, even flaccid. The vampires warn them that Arianna's pussy might prove too much for them since she has the strength inside her cunt of a hundred men. Looking at her, you wouldn't say so. She looks like she has been given far too much of a very good opiate.

There is suddenly an incredible chill on her cunt and then inside it. This chill runs down her thighs and even into her crack. The men are using water to try to clean her cunt from the wolves' semen. It's just a little too much, and even with the strong smell of her pussy, you can't help but notice the lingering smell of dog. So they soak her pussy with the cold water and then run their fingers inside her, moving them around so that they get as much water in and therefore as much semen out, as possible.

The cold has a very interesting effect on her clit. It expands, turning a deep red, and looking like it might just explode. The men can't help giving it a rub with their lips, not yet sure if she is sufficiently cleaned of the wolves to let their tongues explore. They just let their lips settle on the massive clit, perched perfectly above her pussy, and move from side to side and then up and down. Now the smell between Arianna's legs is more pussy than anything else. It's time to have some fun with her now.

Fingers move over her pussy more gently than anyone would have expected given the sight of the hands on her.

The ache deep inside her is almost all consuming and her groin seems to have a million drums beating inside it. Arianna tries to reach for the hand that is moving on her pussy so that she can get at least some of it inside her. But she is bound, just a precaution so that she doesn't manage a bite into one of the humans that are now too close to her than they should be comfortable with. But she knows that she is in no state to start something. And, fever or not, she is caught in an erotic hypnosis that even her need to feed can't free her from.

Finally one of the men has the sense to feed her his fingers. She moans louder than she has and the wolves look up, needing to see what brought this sound from the woman. Three fingers are moving around inside her pussy while others are running circles on her clit. Then there is a single finger in her asshole and Arianna is wriggling like a snake, trying to get more into her. Nobody goes close to her mouth though, none of them are that brave.

Then she feels it. Just the tip of a tongue is on her clit. Again the gentleness is strange given the savage doing the licking. He moves her lips apart and runs his tongue down the center of her pussy, searching for her hole but not trying too hard so that he is again licking delicate circles on her clit again. The others watch, waiting for their turn, rubbing dicks averaging a massive fifteen inches. Then the tongue is inside her vagina and Arianna screams in ecstasy. Again everyone looks to see what has made her so incredibly happy.

The vampires move in, leaving Tanner alone now to watch or not watch. They want to get in close to see just what impact these humans can have on Arianna. It will probably be nothing like the effect they will have, but still, they want to see up close how she will respond to them. It's mostly because their egos will need them to do a hundred times better when the humans are done. The three gather around her head, stroking her face, running fingers along her lips, and then dipping them into her mouth. One of them kisses her, and before she can stop herself, she is kissing him back. Tanner makes a concerted effort to put her behavior down to her fever, and the fact that she has not eaten.

The men take their time, giving each other a turn with their mouths on her pussy. Their tongues go deep now; the more sure they are that there is nothing inside it but Arianna's flow. They sometimes nibble on her clit a little too enthusiastically. Arianna's legs are rubbed and parted and then her thighs squeezed. All this while a head is between them and a mouth is working on her cunt. Her face is stroked while she moans, often not even sure where she is. But then a finger finds her pussy and the pleasure brings her to the present, sort of.

A bulky mass of a man, Rhab, is the first one to take his dick into her. He sends three fingers into her and moves them around gently until they come out sufficiently wet. Then he moves his waist between her legs without getting on top of her so that the others can see. He takes the head of his massive cock and rubs it over her clit briefly. Arianna's clit is on fire. So is her pussy. He moves it between her slit and then gives an easy thrust inward. Half of his cock disappears into her and the others give him a roaring round of applause.

Rhab realizes almost immediately that this isn't going to be like the other pussy he is used to. No sooner has his dick gone into her and it feels like Arianna's cunt is squeezing the shit out of it in powerful milking motions. He sends the rest of his dick into her, hoping to counter this. But his entire shaft is just subjected to this squeeze. He has no choice but to thrust with all the strength in his lower back, despite him having wanted to give his buddies a bit of a show.

He moves all the way in and finds it hard to pull even a little bit of his dick out. Arianna's pussy seems to have taken full possession of it. The squeeze is intense. Rhab tries to thrust harder, to give it a little more, but it doesn't help him. For all his efforts, he is cumming in minutes. Now the applause has been replaced with mockery and laughter.

"Why doesn't one of you give it a go, see how long you can last...?" Rhab is disappointed in himself and also at the fact that this happened in front of a crowd.

Try as they might, none of the others manages to last much longer than Rhab did. Soon enough, nobody is laughing. Well, nobody but the wolves and the vampires. The strain on the humans' faces is visible with long veins from their foreheads down their necks. They must be commended for the effort though. They did try. However, while they managed to give Arianna orgasms with their mouths and their fingers even, their dicks fell short.

The twelve throw themselves on the floor among the wolves, exhausted. This proves too tempting for the dogs who suddenly remember the true nature of things. The vampires too, satisfied that they've made their point with the dozen human dicks in Arianna, can't resist their nature a second longer. The dozen is devoured in minutes, wolf and vampire alike very satisfied. They drop just enough blood on Arianna's lips to keep her present. She salivates at the taste.

Arianna has three vampires now circling her. They have watched her pussy sweat over and over. They have listened to her moan from deep inside herself so that they wish that they were the ones inside her pussy when she was moaning. Tanner knows that there is only one thing that would make this entire situation acceptable for Arianna, and that would be if she wasn't enjoying it the way she is. Since the wolves, then the humans, her pussy has just gone from ecstasy to ecstasy, and there really is nothing that she can do about it. Everyone who touches her pussy just knows exactly what to do.

"You've been very naughty Arianna..." Again she doesn't know who is speaking to her. All she knows from the way they are running their fingers up and down the length of her body is that again she is going to go down the road to erotic satisfaction that will probably hurt Tanner more than he will ever be able to say. This really is the worst kind of punishment, for both of them. The vampires will once again get her to betray herself.

Her pussy is parted so that they can see inside it. It is oozing with semen. They press on her belly and then on the parts of her thigh closest to her cunt. Some of the human seed drains out. It isn't enough. They call on the dogs who had already settled into the show, some of them still nibbling on the leftovers from their meal. One of the wolves goes into Arianna enthusiastically with his tongue, lapping up the contents of her pussy. This gives him an incredible erection; one that he will be able to do nothing about.

"That's enough, dog. Step back..." The vampires have been patient long enough. These three want a decent amount of time with her before the others get her.

The first fingers to go into Arianna's pussy find it very warm. There is a throbbing inside her pussy that the vampire fingering her finds very interesting so that he keeps his fingers lodged deep inside her. This beating moves through his fingers and almost into his arm. This, coupled with the heat, makes him very excited about getting his dick inside her. All the vampires are naked now, and the sight of their cocks is truly magnificent.

They bring their dicks up against Arianna, rubbing them along her legs so that she knows what she is in for. The fever has the surface of her skin as warm as the inside of her cunt so that again the three feel like they have the pleasure of fucking a human. At least this one will last longer than most, they joke. Arianna really has retained most of her human qualities, and she hasn't been a vampire long enough for her to be below room temperature, not yet.

In her delirium, she registers the cock rubbing up against her. She processes the fingers inside her cunt. Her inner beating intensifies, and the fingering becomes insistent. Then more fingers are added to her pussy, and she knows that these are not from the vampire whose fingers are already inside her. Two of them are now fingering her at once. Without warning, the third one sends his tongue into her mouth. He moves it around inside her so that his tongue cools her saliva. Then he rubs his balls against her lips while fondling her perfect breasts.

There is not a part of Arianna's body that is not tingling now. It's almost like very intense erotic tremors. She knows that with these men, it is very quickly going to become an earthquake, their power is now a more than competent match for her own. One thing for sure too, vampires know how to handle vampires, even turned ones. And there is nothing about the inside of Arianna's pussy that will be a surprise for these three. They know what to expect. And they know just what to do with it.

The fingers inside her are almost overwhelming. It's as if the pair can't decide what instrument they want to play, so they just play every single one. They seem to be conducting an orchestra inside Arianna's pussy that already has her murmuring as her cunt starts dripping from within. Even if she wanted to, she can't think of Tanner now. Vampires have a way of making fucking an all-consuming event. Arianna can be nowhere else right now except putty in the evil hands of the three determined to enjoy her before they hand her over to The Leadership. Despite her fever, her exhaustion, and what is now bordering dangerously on starvation, there is no doubt that she too will enjoy every second of it.

"You must remember me as Luther..." one of the vampires is sure to let Arianna know who he is. The egos on them are really something else. It fuels their sex drive just the thought that while they work on her, she will know their names. Arianna doesn't respond.

He comes down even closer, his mouth practically inside her ear. Then he sends his tongue into her ear and licks around the entire inside of it. Afterward, he licks the outside of it and introduces himself to her again. This time as he says his name, he moves his fingers into her cunt, the others having stepped aside so that he can do his thing. He manages to get four fingers deep inside Arianna before he is satisfied that she knows who he is.

Then he removes the fingers slowly and lets them run under Arianna's nose so that she smells herself. After letting her know, he takes the fingers into his mouth and sucks the liquid left there by Arianna's pussy. Then Luther is inside her again, repeating the exercise a few times until he has quenched his thirst for the juices of her pussy, and until he is happy that it is wet and ready for his sword. He runs his hand up the length of his dick and then points it toward Arianna's waiting snatch.

The others watch as he can't hold back from getting

inside her now. Every inch of his dick moves all the way into Arianna, who murmurs with delight. Luther goes all the way in so that his balls are connected to the outside of her pussy. Then he pulls out a little before thrusting back in. Even when he tries to measure his thrusting it is so powerful that Arianna moves almost completely off the makeshift bed. The other two hold her in place, lending their buddy a hand.

Arianna closes her eyes, trying to go back to her special place with Tanner. But she can't. Not now. She can't, not even for a second, pretend that the power between her thighs is human. She can't imagine that it is anything but vampires in the room. And this is just the first one. This is what they want. They want her to acknowledge that only they know what to do with her pussy. Even if she won't say it out loud. They will make sure that it is more than obvious.

Luther fucks Arianna in perfect strokes while the others hold her in place. She has an orgasm first and then he goes at her harder so that he too can get there. Still, it seems to take him forever. But there is no way that he will move his dick from where it is without emptying it first. The others know this. The wolves watch eagerly as the thrusting gets more and more aggressive and Arianna seems like she might have another orgasm. The ground seems to shake under the determined thrusting until eventually Luther lets out a strange mix of hissing and grunting as he empties his cock into Arianna.

Maximilian doesn't even need to ask the wolves to clear Arianna's pussy of Luther's jizz. Already the dogs are licking the inside of her cunt so that not a trace of it is left. The thick wet tongues cool down the inside of Arianna's pussy and then immediately set it on fire again so that all she wants is to be fucked. Her eyes remain shut constantly now as she convinces herself that this is all just a dream.

Then Max is on her clean cunt. The wolves find their place on the ground again and attend to their own erections. He takes a moment to let his nose settle in her curls so that he can take a deep whiff. Then he moves into her with his tongue and warms her pussy up even further. Arianna doesn't even try to resist him. She surrenders so completely that soon enough Max is drinking her excessive wetness.

When he inserts his cock into her she shivers. He goes in so slowly that Arianna is momentarily confused as the moment seems suddenly to be suspended. Max watches his own dick disappearing into her and then watches as her breasts start to form more glistening beads of sweat. He moves into her deep and then starts an almost ritualistic motion in measured circles. The sounds coming from Arianna keep sending unexpected signals to Tanner's dick and it goes hard often until he reminds himself of the situation.

Max is not as controlled as Luther, who kept going steadily without skipping a beat. His circles vary in size and then he is just thrusting hard in and out of her cunt. Then long slow thrusts are followed again by quick short ones. Then he drops his mouth onto hers, sends his tongue into her mouth, and just moves his dick rapidly from side to side in her pussy. Arianna pulls on her restraints not because she thinks she can get away, but because she is losing her mind from ecstasy and isn't even aware that she is doing it.

Just looking at her drives Max crazy, himself. Luther is already sporting another erection. But he's going to have to be patient if he wants another go. Max is almost done and there is one dick that is practically dripping now, keen to get between Arianna's perfect thighs. Max has his tongue in her mouth again, her spit warming his while his cools hers. His circles are not as wide as they've been in her cunt but they are much more intense. Only once he begins his orgasm does he move his mouth from hers. He too hisses as he climaxes, and keeps fucking her until she has an orgasm that fuses loudly with his. Now Max is satisfied.

The temperature of Arianna's body fluctuates now and she starts to look like she might have a seizure. The third vampire comes in close to her face and kisses her on the lips. There is a familiarity with these lips that pulls Arianna from wherever she is and she opens her eyes. It's still hard to see, the salt from the sweat flowing into her eyes from her brow making it painful to even try. Then he speaks.

"I've waited for you for a very long time Arianna..." His voice drives her insane. She can't imagine that she wants him. She can't imagine that there is anything that he can do to make her body want him. She tries hard to imagine who he is as again he speaks directly into her ear before kissing her on her neck with such tenderness that she almost wants to pull him closer. There is a lapping up of Max between her legs and she knows that it won't be long before this third vampire too will be coating the inside of her pussy.

He holds her legs apart and gives her pussy an almost affectionate look. Then his fingers move into her and he moves them in small circles inside Arianna, checking for tightness. Her pussy doesn't disappoint, having remained remarkably tight throughout the lust fest. It's going to be as tight for him as it was for the first wolf.

There is no need to drag it out. His cock goes into her so that her pussy moves out in all directions. Again Arianna is pulling on her restraints, suddenly needing to pull this cock deeper into her. Tanner watches her wanting this viper on her, wanting him inside her. The vampire doesn't even pretend like he's not going to give her exactly what she wants.

His dick is inside her and his thrusting is perfect. Arianna knows that many humans have fallen foul of this perfect cock that seems to be dealing quite well with her pussy. She wraps her cunt tightly around the dick that is moving with incredible precision and already she is producing copious amounts of her own lava. The speed with which this third cock has started to pull orgasms from her takes her by as much surprise as it does Max and Luther, who look on enviously.

Still, he doesn't stop. Using nothing but his dick in well-thought-out strokes, he practically has a river flowing from Arianna's pussy and down her thighs. He watches, impressed by what he alone has managed to do with nothing but his dick. He is close now, and the others come in for a closer look as they sense his impending explosion. It is going to be epic.

Finally, as he cums inside her, and as her own juices mix with his, suddenly Arianna remembers who he is. She can't say his name out loud, sheer exhaustion. But she does manage a whisper.

"Credo..." she says, and then passes out completely for the first time.

CHAPTER 8

EVERYONE in the cave is now completely taken over by the fucking. Those who are fucking are obsessed. The woman being fucked is just caught up in orgasm after perfect orgasm. The audience is oblivious to anything outside of itself, or the cave. The whole world is now just one orgy, lulling them into an erotic paradise that has them almost forgetting how this will end for Arianna and Tanner.

Only Tanner has managed to retain some sort of awareness. He has seen the night become day and then night again. He has seen that it is raining, still, and that they are not as deep in the earth as he had thought. Tanner knows that the outside of the cave is real. He isn't sure though, especially given his distance from the mouth of the cave, and the fact that tonight is darker than usual if he caught the outline of a shepherd's staff near the entrance.

Memories of his brother in their younger days flood his head. Tanner must be hallucinating. It must be all the blood that he's lost. But then a flash of lightning and again the outline of a shepherd's staff can be seen. There seem to appear one or two more. This can't be. And when more vampires arrive, accompanied by a pair of wolves, Tanner knows that it cannot be true. Surely if his brother and his friends were in fact outside, they would be dead by now. And the vampires and wolves would not hesitate to let them know of the kill, just to taunt them. But there are no signs on wolves or vampires of a feed.

"So this is her little lover..." Karl is a particularly vile vampire, one of the heads of the Leadership's Guard.

Nobody answers, just laughing as Karl's hands move all over Tanner's body and then he sticks a finger deep into one of his wounds so that Tanner screams out loud.

"And has he enjoyed watching his little princess having her precious pussy taken to task by men who are up to it?" Still, Karl is taunting Tanner, not really expecting a response, the evidence speaking for itself. Then he makes his way to Arianna, who for the first time is without a penis in her pussy. This brings her back from her sex-induced euphoria and her focus is momentarily on Tanner again.

But then Karl has his fingertips along the slit separating Arianna's pussy. And almost immediately her focus is on her own body again. Karl is able to undress himself with just one hand while keeping his other hand on Arianna, exploring the body that has been massively explored already. Soon enough he is completely naked, with everyone looking at his incredibly powerful body, his erection well past his naval in a gentle curve.

He runs his erection along with the warmth of Arianna's legs. The thunder outside sounds like there must be one hell of a storm on the go. But it does provide the perfect accompaniment to the beating between Arianna's legs as each stroke from Karl's fingers fires her up so that she wants him inside her also. The other vampires look at his impressive cock and know that this is going to be a definite piece de resistance. Karl has been a vampire for longer than most and is definitely the one to watch.

There is no urgency as everyone takes in the sounds of the storm and plays casually with their own dicks. Many of them wish that there were a few more Ariannas in the cave. That would have made it quite a party. The Leadership has also put a limit on the festivities, wanting them to get Arianna back to them as soon as possible, the possibility of her being delivered alive too irresistible for them. So Karl knows that he is going to be one of the last to get inside her. The others might have a go again on the journey back. Tanner isn't needed at the headquarters so they'll probably just leave him with the wolves.

Karl has taken stock of the situation and so he removes all the bonds on Arianna. There isn't much that she can do in terms of attacking him. He wipes the sweat from her brow and then runs a little water over her chest to clear the sweat there. The water travels straight down between her thighs and runs through her pubic hairs. Karl's fingers are soon moving the water around the soft curls and then on the inside of her pussy which he finds a little slippery.

More water on her cunt directly and Karl is working on the inside of Arianna's snatch, cleaning it of all liquid. Her cunt has never needed to be cleaned so often before. The wolves look on, wondering why their licking services aren't being employed. Karl needs no help when it comes to handling a vagina. He will thoroughly prepare it for himself, and then thoroughly enjoy it by himself.

He is soon happy that Arianna is clean enough for him. Karl settles his mouth over her moist breast, holding her up. He has her one arm over his neck and has her facing Tanner directly. Tanner watches as Karl moves his lips from breast to breast. He watches how Arianna's fingers go instinctively between her legs and then how she tries to keep herself from falling over as she is overcome by lust.

Tanner watches Karl's fingers moving up and down over Arianna's belly and then settling on her clit. He watches as she loses her balance as Karl works on her bean. He is so painfully slow and deliberate about it that just watching him creates a strange tension in the cave. Nobody speaks. Many of them hardly breathe. They are all suddenly unsure of how to touch their cocks. Everything is now about Karl and Arianna.

"I'm about to make all your dreams come true..." Karl whispers in her ear.

He uses the palm of his hand to rub the hairy surface of her cunt. Then he uses just his finger to slide between her slit. Then he pinches her clit between two of his fingers and gives it a gentle pull. After a while, he just taps it with the tip of his finger as she begs for him to enter her. Karl will be inside her soon enough. For now, he is enjoying Tanner's reaction to his performance almost as much as he is enjoying Arianna's feverish reaction to his touch.

Karl teases the inside of her pussy with just the tip of his finger. It's quite a strong tip. Arianna almost squirms. Her legs move apart so that the inside of her thighs is clearly visible. Again Tanner can't help an erection. His cock goes full mast as Karl makes his way into Arianna with a little more of his finger. Even when he tries to look away now, the images are just too clear in his head that his erection is going nowhere. The wolves whistle and the vampires give him and his hard dick mock applause.

With absolutely zero effort Karl rises off the ground, Arianna in hand. Then he hovers in a reclining position so that her legs hang on either side of him. Now he can move around slowly for the viewing benefit of all in the space. But his focus is mainly on Tanner. Karl now really digs into her pussy with his fingers, his cock perfectly snug between her ass cheeks, the head in contact with her lower back. He grates against her warm crack while drawing massive amounts of moisture from her pussy.

Then he has both hands on her breasts and everyone watches as her nipples harden and swell. Her breasts seem to swell too. Karl plays Arianna like an erotic instrument that only he has mastered, and with every touch, with every tug, he pulls from her the most erotic sounds. She is completely under his spell, so much so that nothing else exists for her now.

Karl positions Arianna on his belly and then places his cock in direct line with her pussy. Then he creates the slightest diagonal so that she slips perfectly onto his dick, midair, and everyone watches as the full shaft finds the inside of Arianna's pussy, hanging her on Karl's dick just off the ground. Then Karl takes hold of her breasts and continues to fondle them while Arianna adjusts to his cock inside her. He too is making the adjustment as her pussy starts its squeezing action on his cock almost immediately.

As the muscles in Arianna's vagina ripple up and down his shaft, Karl has to do nothing but enjoy the power of her cunt. He handles her breasts with one hand while taking care of her clit with the other. All the while he hovers just off the floor so that he hangs the show just high enough for all to see. Tanner can't help but watch now either, his cock dripping jizz from the thick tip.

It's hard to resist the urge to thrust into Arianna's cunt. Karl manages to for an impressive amount of time though. But then even he can't. He takes the hand that is working on her clit and places it firmly on the inside of her one thigh. Then he slides her up his dick just enough to allow him to then let her drop back down while he thrusts up. He does this over and over again, building up his urges to really fuck the shit out of this beautiful pussy. For a moment he wishes it was just him and her and the Leadership wasn't waiting to get her to ensure that she stopped making a nuisance of herself.

In fact, now that they've been inside her pussy, everyone seems to have forgotten why they had been so aggressively pursuing Arianna. They seem to have now forgotten that she was getting in the way of their feeding, their fucking, and their fun. None of them seems to be aware of the fact anymore that this should be punishment for her and not pleasure. But they do know that once they're done, and she realizes who and what has moved through her, that will be punishment enough. Then the Leadership can dispose of her and life can go back to normal.

Karl removes his cock from her completely and lays her on the mud bed. Some of those on the ground stand as soon as it becomes clear that in the position they're in, they will soon not be able to see what is happening. He moves her lips apart with his fingers, hovering above her now so that his head is above her cunt, and his cock is over her mouth. Holding her pussy lips apart with his fingertips, he sends his tongue into her hole, while maneuvering his cock into her mouth. She sucks on it enthusiastically almost immediately, the heat in her mouth from her growing fever making his cock very happy.

While paying careful attention to her pussy with his own mouth, he fucks Arianna's mouth with the full length of his dick. He slides his dick all the way into her throat, lets it settle there for a moment, and then pulls the locked cock back out. Arianna doesn't even flinch. Karl is so good at fucking her throat that she just takes the entire mass into her over and over again while his tongue goes as deep into her pussy as possible, lapping up the walls of her cunt hard. She sprays a load into his mouth that has him settle his head completely between her legs and suck as much of her lava into him as possible. Still, his dick glides in and out of her windpipe, turning her mouth into a makeshift vagina.

Then Karl moves his cock from her throat and is fucking the main part of her mouth. The saliva there is so warm that he feels the urge to dunk his massive nuts into her mouth. But Arianna is a little too out of it to be any good at trying to make that happen. He can't imagine her opening her mouth if he asked her, no matter how good he was making her pussy feel. He has four fingers in her cunt now so that it is almost breathing into his hand. The beating of her clitoris is almost visible, the vibration almost audible.

He's never been one not to at least try to get what he wants. Karl is known for making the impossible possible. He moves his erection out of the heat of Arianna's mouth and then runs his shaft over her face. He lets his balls settle on and then rub against her cheeks while his tongue is inside her pussy again. Then his sack is on her lips and he is mimicking with his mouth over her pussy what he wants her to do with her mouth over his nuts.

Sure enough her lips start to part. Then her teeth separate and there is enough space between them for Karl to drop his sack into the melting pot that is Arianna's mouth. After making some adjustments, his entire sack is inside her mouth, wet with her spit, her tongue moving over his balls while her mouth creates just enough suction to keep Karl's balls in place. He rewards her by sending thick fingers into her cunt while rapidly licking her clit so that she has several orgasms in quick succession.

He can leave his sack in her mouth forever, it feels so

fucking good. But there is the risk that the audience might get restless. It is starting to feel like Karl is showing off. And the show can only continue as long as he keeps the others entertained. So Karl decides to just move things along so that he can at least have an orgasm. After that, he couldn't give a fuck who does what with whom. Reluctantly he lifts his sack from Arianna's mouth.

Again he aligns his cock with her cunt, settling his head at exactly the place where the folds cover her snatch. He moves between them and soon he is driving his cock into her, an inch at a time. She murmurs, Karl wiping more sweat from her brow before digging a finger and then two into her mouth just to tease himself with the thought of this warmth. He fingers her mouth, enjoying the spit on his fingers. The same warmth is on his cock as he now makes full entry and thrusts steadily.

His ass rises very high into the air behind him as he makes accommodation for every inch of his cock. Then he goes down deep and hard so that again all of him is inside her. Again she is an instrument and the sounds coming from her have turned everyone on incredibly, including Tanner, and again they are confused as to the pace at which they should be touching their dicks, not sure if they would rather hold on until Karl finishes, and deal with this arousal inside her cunt. It's a fiery magnificent powerful cunt. It would be an incredible waste to settle for just one round. They all wish now that they'd had the same restraint as Karl so that they could have made their rounds last as long.

Watching Karl on Arianna is a fucking magnificent sight. He glides over her, up and down and then in circles, lifting up so that he seems to want to hook her with his dick and raise her into her air. He does this often, getting very close to lifting her with just his dick. Then he settles back down and just resumes fucking. The others aren't sure if they want him to stop or not, Karl giving them an incredible lesson in how to fuck a vampire.

Then he holds her to him and wraps his legs around her completely. With her cunt locked against his cock now, he plows into her. Rapid circles send fire into her pussy so that she is moaning on each stroke. Her cunt is wet and Karl holds her to him tightly with just the muscles of his legs, no time to try to dry out her pussy. Arianna can still feel every part of his dick on every single part of her pussy, so her wetness is not a problem for her at all.

His dick is really reaching places none before it had. This is more than Arianna thought possible, especially given the excesses of the wolves. But Karl is proving that it really isn't the size of the stick, but the skill of the beating. He moves his circles faster, lifting them off the ground before going in and out in a perfect straight line over and over again. He brings her close to another massive orgasm and then pulls her back by breaking the rhythm and pausing for just a single beat. Every time he does this Arianna is screaming for him to fuck her harder. The sound of this takes Tanner to a dream he'd much sooner forget.

By the time Karl has Arianna back on her throne, he has unwrapped his legs. Arianna's are shuddering from all the power that has been moving between them. Karl digs his fingers gently into her muscles, from her ankles all the way back up to her cunt, getting her circulation going and restoring her to some extent. His dick never leaves the inside of her as he does, and soon enough Arianna is trying to wrap herself around Karl as another orgasm approaches.

Everyone watches as Karl just gets his shit right again and again. Still no orgasm from him, but each one he summons from Arianna is beautiful to watch. Every dick in the semi-darkness is now aching for her pussy. Every single one of them wants a chance to outdo Karl. They all know that this might just prove impossible. Even Credo has already conceded defeat in his head. This doesn't mean he wouldn't like a second dip though. But Karl isn't letting anyone near Arianna, not until he himself is done.

He reaches his hands under her ass and gives her butt a firm squeeze. It's a tight, firm muscle and this shoots pleasure right into his balls. He presses her cunt against him by pushing up her ass and settles deeper inside her with his cock. His thrusts are now complete movements into her and half movements out. He really needs to cum now. After every dozen or so thrusts like this, he gives her cunt half a dozen powerful circular strokes. Arianna has an earth-shattering orgasm and then starts to shake uncontrollably. Everyone comes in close now, convinced that Karl might actually be managing to fuck Arianna to death.

But he doesn't. He takes a deep breath and keeps going, getting himself closer and closer to orgasm by going deeper and deeper into Arianna. He forgets about everyone around him and doesn't allow the pressure of the stares to have any effect on him. He has impressed, no doubt. Now he can just make it all about him. He rubs his dick hard against every side of Arianna's pussy as it continues to sweat a continuous flow.

Finally, he pulls his dick from her and turns her over. He uses his palm to remove the slippery stickiness and then rubs some of it on her asshole. This is the only way that he is going to cum now. The others salivate at the thought. They all beat on their dicks aggressively as Karl moves his cock into Arianna's chocolate box to the deepest moaning from both of them. Tanner bows his head, ashamed for the millionth time by his erection.

Now Karl is thrusting furiously. He makes Arianna almost arch all the way back each time he thrusts all the way in. Then he takes hold of both her arms and pulls her back so that she forms an S, her breasts shooting out in front of her as her ass comes up high to meet the dick it's being fed. Karl really digs into her, the curve of his cock working perfectly with this position. Arianna is burning up so much now though that for the first time, even Karl thinks he might lose her. This might be a problem now of course, the Leadership having stated now that they would prefer it if she was delivered alive.

But vampires are generous when it comes to cunt. So they want to give as many as can get here a go inside this wonderful Eden. Arianna's cunt really is a cross between the Promised Land and paradise. It works whatever magic a dick is working on it right back at it, times a thousand. And one can only imagine how much more intense this must be when she is at full strength and not being killed slowly by werewolf saliva.

Karl can think of nothing else now but shooting the massive load that has been building up inside him for almost half a day. The length of his strokes shortens considerably and the pace quickens. He looks almost as though he too now is overcome with a strange fever. He starts to hiss, saliva falling from the side of his mouth, his fangs fully protruding. He is in the land of no return. His dick moves madly inside Arianna's asshole now and he pulls her back toward him with all his strength, threatening to snap her arms right off. Just in time though, he convulses madly and starts to rain semen through his cock and deposit it all quite neatly inside Arianna's asshole. His hissing and grunting sound like he is in the throws of an incredible battle.

Meanwhile outside the darkness again consumes the

world. The vampires come out into the stormy night, needing to find food, not wanting it to be Tanner just yet. Besides, one man wouldn't be enough for all the vampires in the cave. Unknown to them, they pass seven healthy young shepherds, so close to the mouth of the cave, hidden in the underbrush of the clearing just beyond, that they should be able to smell them. But between the continuous rain lifting heavy smells of earth and plant life, and the rotting wolf hides that the seven have all but wrapped themselves in, the vampires, and even the wolves that come out to feed, move right passed them. Arianna and Tanner are never left alone though, so rescue won't be simple. The shepherds will have to give themselves some more time to figure out how to save Tanner, the only reason Luke and his friends would be risking their lives like this.

Inside the cave, there is a strange silence now. There is nothing that Tanner and Arianna are aware of now more than they are of the repetitive rapping of the rain on the earth and rocks outside. They've stopped thinking about escape. Their heads are filled with the good things that they have done or tried to do in their lives. This comforts them both in what they believe is their final hours.

If only they could look at each other. If only they could touch each other, just once. This is not possible. The only person able to touch them is the vampire left in the cave with them to keep guard. Maybe the wolves too if the vampire allows to pair a go. It doesn't matter to them. All they know is that for Tanner whatever the touching is will mean pain, and hopefully death. For Arianna, it will mean another orgasm that she would regret for the rest of her life if she wasn't sure that she wouldn't be alive for much longer.

There is still a heavy erotic air in the space. The

appetites have been filled to some extent by the quick feed that they had so their strength is up and they can give Arianna another go. They contemplate it but she isn't looking too well. There is the temptation to feed her, just a little, to keep her alive. There is too much of a risk though so they decide against it. Arianna is fading though. Tanner has held on remarkably well but he too is starting to give up the fight.

The wolves settle for touching themselves and licking their own balls. This amuses the vampire but he too has a hand on his dick and is giving it lengthy strokes. The temptation is starting to build and Arianna's pussy is again at risk. It's so vulnerable and beautiful that it seems that it won't be long before someone is in there again. The smell of the work that it's put in hangs in the air and makes the temptation almost unbearable.

CHAPTER 9

THE WIND BLOWS straight into the cave now and directly against Tanner, almost as though it was sent directly to him. Every part of his naked body is now beaten by the icy breeze, and Tanner succumbs to the massive loss of blood, losing consciousness completely for the first time. In his unconscious state, his mind is free to wander...

There is nothing and no one in the cave now except for Tanner and Arianna. She is still naked, and so is he. But their bodies are in perfect order with no exhaustion and no wounds, and Arianna's pussy is fresh and beautiful. Tanner and Arianna listen to the storm outside, the night wild and sexy; and inside the cave, Tanner has managed a roaring fire. With the warmth inside, the storm outside is every bit as magical as a storm should be. Adding to this are thick, cleaned werewolf furs strewn across the ground. In his mind, Tanner has done the killing, cleaning, and preparation of this perfectly acceptable Bartholomew-type bed.

The embrace feels like they are hugging inside the center of the flames. Tanner watches as the flames dance in shadows up and down their bodies. It's exactly as it needs to be. His hardness is proof that there isn't a single element of the scenario that is out of place. He accepts his arousal, brought on by the beautiful woman in his arms, and his yearning that is almost an aching for every part of her.

Tanner places his lips on Arianna's and their tongues join immediately. Love and lust fuse perfectly in their mouths and make the journey to every part of their bodies. There is no doubt where this will go, or how. Both of them almost lose their ability to think as they drop in slow motion to the ground. There is absolutely no reason now for anything to make any sort of sense.

Arianna's goosebumps are so prominent that Tanner can run his fingertips along with individual ones. Each time he does, she seems to lose her breath. He places his lips on the surface of her skin and this too overwhelms her. She takes her own fingertips to his scrotum and gently moves over the entire surface of his balls. His erection isn't easy to ignore either.

Lying side by side on the warmth of the furs both of them are tempted to roll onto one another. But they need access to the parts of each other that the current position allows. So side by side it is. Mouths meet again and the connection between the pair is sealed. Tongues lock and all emotion is confirmed. They couldn't be any closer now if Tanner's throbbing erection was already inside her, fused erotically to her willing vagina.

Tanner finds the roof of Arianna's mouth with his tongue, sending her into an incredible giggle that fills the entire space. The sound is deeply comforting. He does it again, her happiness almost tangible for him. He loves it. He loves her. Then he searches the rest of her mouth before resuming the tongue tango that sees them pull deeper into one another. It feels like Tanner is touching her heart with the passion of his kisses. And she is letting him into every part of her.

When he finally places himself on top of her he separates her legs with his frame. As he bends his legs at the knees, her legs move a little further apart. He sends his hand between them and places his palm over her pussy just to feel the warmth lifting off it. Then he places his hand on it directly and allows this heat to move from inside her cunt onto his hand. It seems to dance along each of his fingers and then wrap itself on his wrist. Then he moves his hand back up the side of her body and places it on her breast.

He moves his mouth from one of Arianna's breasts to the other and back again, almost as though he can't make up his mind as to which one tastes better. Tanner settles on each one for the longest time trying to decide. Then he takes the tip of his tongue to her nipples and again Arianna fills the space with laughter. She likes to be tickled. But she also hates it. Tanner finds this strange and amusing and very endearing.

When the tip of his tongue is drawing a clear line down her belly Arianna goes wild with the anticipation of Tanner's tongue's destination. He doesn't keep her in anticipation too long. Finding her clit, he gives it abnormally quick licks and then laps up the moisture it produces with an incredible slowness that is almost painful. Then he is licking quickly again and Arianna is dripping love juice from parts of her pussy he hasn't even touched yet.

Her legs are now comfortably around his neck as he starts to make a meal of her pussy. He eats her out with such gentleness, such passion that even if this was all he did for the rest of her life it would be more than she needed. In fact, it would be more than she could handle. He goes at her punani as though he just might do it forever. Again she is dripping *into his mouth, quenching every single one of Tanner's thirsts.*

Tanner is salivating when he gets his mouth back up to Arianna's. The contents of his mouth drops onto her lips and she licks it into her mouth. Then he joins their lips and moves his fingers back down between her legs. The warm wetness is too much for him to resist and Tanner positions his hardness directly on the moisture. Arianna inhales and Tanner exhales as he moves into her slowly, filling her completely in a single, calculated stroke.

Their bodies glide across the furs, up and down. They move into each other from their hearts more than anything else and the emotion of their lovemaking elevates it to an almost spiritual level. In and out of her, Tanner fills her with each stroke. Arianna receives him into every part of her while working her own femininity on his erection so that Tanner's heaven is also complete and clearly marked.

There is a sense of forever in dreams that makes an orgasm seem like an intrusion, so neither of them works toward one. They simply indulge themselves in one another, each of them the other's sole purpose. Nothing can bring them from this paradise in Tanner's head. Even death right now would be a most pleasant thing for Tanner, who has really only managed to make real physical love with Arianna in his dreams.

So his dreams are where he chooses to stay...

While Arianna's fever now has her delusional in the real world, the world inside her head is clearer than anything that has ever been real to her before. And in this reality, Tanner is everything she needs him to be. He has become everything she wants him to be...

So vivid is her own recreation of Tanner that she can trace the path of his veins over his perfectly sculpted body.

She can see every part of his skin and find it with the parts of herself she chooses. She chooses her fingers mostly so that she can observe his reaction to her. Arianna wets the tips of her fingers and works up and down the length of Tanner's arousal. Then she wets them some more and explores his bulging scrotum. Each time she touches him his entire penis pulses, jerking to the side.

Then Arianna wraps her mouth over the top of it. She lets the warmth settle on the tip before sliding down more and more of the long love tool. She gets so much of it into her mouth that every time she parts her lips to exhale, she shrouds Tanner's balls in a cloud of warm air. He loves this. After just a few movements of her mouth up and down the shaft, Arianna is managing all of it in her mouth.

Tanner runs his fingers through her hair. He settles his fingertips on her scalp and massages her head while she massages his dick with her mouth. She moves her fingers into herself and imagines Tanner inside her. Her movements in her pussy are powerful and every bit conducive with the feeling and texture of the cock in her mouth. This connection lulls Arianna deeper and deeper into the world that is her creation and she builds slowly and progressively toward the penetration she craves but is in no hurry to get to in the eternity that is her imagination...

Credo is standing guard, a few wolves at the entrance too as a strange tension starts to overwhelm them. He is watching Arianna as she responds in the real world to whatever is going on in her mind. He looks at Tanner who, despite his unconsciousness, has a massive erection that is nothing like the limpness of his body as he hangs from his stake. If it wasn't for the ropes holding him up under his arms, he would have fallen to the ground by now. He is bleeding slowly now and Credo knows that if he is going to get a decent drink from him, it would have to be soon. But his attention is on the moaning of Arianna who has managed to find the inside of her pussy with her fingers.

"You dogs watch that entrance. Something is feeling a little off." Credo's senses have always been good but with all the sex he's been having, and the sex he now wants to have, he just feels generally uneasy. Nothing has yet settled over him regarding the shepherds outside.

He goes to Arianna and gently moves her hand from between her legs. She shivers and tries in vain to get back onto her pussy. Credo places his mouth over her hot clit and licks it. Then he sucks on it with such power that he draws the liquid from deep inside her into his mouth. She tastes better now than she did the first time and Credo's dick is rock hard immediately. He can't resist stealing just one more round before the others get back. The wolves are obvious about their envy and dissatisfaction.

"Fuck off..." Credo hisses, and then puts his mouth back on the juicy vagina, going into her with the thickest parts of his tongue.

He mounts Arianna and is inside her quickly. He thrusts slowly, the fire from her and the cool steel of his cock combining so that Credo is the one shaking. Such power is something he has never experienced. He can't imagine that he will ever experience it again once she is handed over to The Leadership. So he makes every effort to really indulge his scepter, dipping deep and fucking her hard. But he doesn't fuck her fast, every stroke too fucking fantastic to waste. Every muscle in his ass moves his dick completely and directly into Arianna, touching every part of her that is being touched in her head. Somewhere in the back of his mind, he remembers Karl.

Credo parts her legs so that he can watch himself

moving in and out of Arianna. It looks every bit as good as it feels. The wolves edge closer, also wanting to see. This is a show that does everything to restore every erection around. Without saying it out loud, everyone admits just how beautiful Arianna is. If she wasn't just so tolerant and protective of humans. They might all just have gotten along very nicely. Sessions like this could just as well have become a regular thing.

It feels as though Arianna has been set on fire. This sensation of permeating warmth is what has made humans such attractive lovers to wolves and vampires. It's something that is unfamiliar to them but works an amazing set of wonders on their dicks. Credo is letting go fast of the anxiety of losing Arianna any time now. He knows that the others will be back from their feed. And then they will have to take her and Tanner to the Leadership. Then there will be no hope for this snug cock wrap that she has between her legs.

So he just keeps sending himself into her. He tries to revive her a little, wanting at least a little bit of involvement from her. All he wants is for her to know that it is him in there. Ego is again at play and Credo can't help himself. He taps the side of her face a little and then removes some of the sweat from her brow. Then he places his mouth on hers and sends his tongue into her mouth. Her lips are very, very warm.

Then Credo kisses her neck. It too is invitingly warm. He almost can't believe himself, the tenderness that is coming from him. He needs to enjoy her. He needs her to enjoy him. This is what he now knows to be the need to make love, the beauty of it. If only Arianna's mortality didn't loom in the air along with everyone's arousal.

The wolves are closer to Credo than he is comfortable,

not because they're watching him, but because they are not watching the entrance. But he is also too consumed with what he is doing now to pay them too much mind. His penis moves comfortably all the way into the back of her vagina now and although he knows they are not for him, she is moaning loudly on each one of his thrusts. The werewolves are masturbating vigorously now, wanting to cum from the show in case Credo is serious about not letting them into her pussy.

Arianna's cunt is getting tighter and tighter. It's also getting wetter and wetter, so Credo goes for her depths a little harder, needing slightly more traction, something that will only happen if he thrusts a little harder. This makes him feel like he is going to cum though and so again he slows down. After a while, he realizes that there is only one way to end this with a bang. He takes his dick out of her pussy slowly and then turns her onto her belly. Then he moves his cock into her ass, tight and not as wet.

Now he resumes his long strokes, no need for hard fucking. He holds her breasts and pulls her to him as he grinds the inside of her ass with his dick. The wolves are very excited when Credo brings her to standing so that they can get on their knees and take whiffs of her dripping pussy. Credo lets them enjoy themselves, as long as they don't get so enthusiastic that they upset his rhythm.

The wolves know that they are on borrowed time so they go at it cautiously. They lick the outside of Arianna's pussy, wanting to go in but first needing to get into Credo's groove. He is giving her ass a good working, his strong hands on her breasts keeping her upright. The wolves start to send their tongues into her tentatively, still pulling on their own dicks, but not as aggressively. Then one of them stands up and meets Credo's eyes. He moves in closer before getting confirmation and sends his cock into the waiting pussy.

Now Arianna is being double-fucked and she comes to her senses for the briefest moments. The wolves get themselves off while Credo still seems no closer to climax. But there is an eerie silence now from outside that makes Credo want to finish up. The rain has stopped. And it's almost dawn. So the vampires will be here anytime now. Credo can't do anything but fuck Arianna's ass hard now that the wolves have cum, and gone. He goes for it aggressively, grateful for Arianna's erotic moaning, which helps him to an epic orgasm...

"This might be our chance...our only chance..." The urgency in Luke's voice carries with his shivers. All seven of them watch as some of the vampires return, a few wolves too.

No sooner have the vampires disappeared into the cave and the sun starts to rise. But this sunrise is not just a lightning of the night into a wet, dreary day. The sun is an orange orb that is blazing into the morning so that it is clear that the vampires are now stuck inside the cave until the sun goes away again. They just need to strategize about the wolves, who have no issues with sunlight.

The only thing about the fact that it's been raining for so long there is nothing dry around them that they can set on fire. All they have are their emergency vats of oil. But they can't use these until they know just how many wolves they will be dealing with. Luke is however anxious about his brother and wants to get him out, no matter what.

The shepherds keep the wolf skins on as they approach the entrance to the cave. There is no time like the present. They know that they are close enough now for the vampires and wolves to be able to smell them now. Even through their disguises, they know that it's not going to be hard to make them out in the absence of the rain.

But this is no time to pull back. They've counted eight wolves, and half a dozen vampires. They can do this. The shepherds get their torches oiled and then place some oil on either end of the entrance to the cave. They light up the entrance to the cave and the wind carries the smoke into the cave almost immediately. Luke takes two of his friends and they storm the smoky darkness, hoping for the best.

He finds his brother and unties him while the vampires try to make sense of fire and wolves. The smoke has them a little confused because they aren't sure who is wolf. Luke knows this won't be for long because the vampires will know that there is no way that the wolves will be holding torches with flames at their end. The wolves can't help fleeing the cave, the smoke and flames forcing this. The vampires are starting to figure it out.

But Luke has passed his torch to one of the others. Then he manages to get Tanner out with the wolves escaping. They go straight to the center of the other shepherds with flaming torches who are already being circled by the wolves who have now all made it out of the cave. The shepherds that entered the cave are with them now, leaving nothing but vampires to deal with the smoke and ever-increasing heat inside the cave. Arianna has been forgotten by all but Tanner. Actually, the shepherds had no intention of saving her.

"Arianna...I must get Arianna..." Tanner manages nothing else. He just keeps saying her name over and over.

"To hell with that vampire bitch, we came here for you brother..." Luke lets Tanner drop to the ground so that he can help the others keep the wolves at bay. The wolves are circling, watching the flames get smaller and smaller, and waiting for them to lose the only protection they have.

The wolves have gotten close enough a few times to get their coats singed. The shepherds have discarded their wolf skins too now, setting them on fire just so that the wolves are taken aback further by the smell of themselves burning. It works. The wolves pull back a little, but not before they've managed to claw a few of the shepherds, drawing blood. This drives the vampires in the cave crazy.

Inside the cave, the vampires realize that they may just be in a little more trouble than they thought. The cave is filling with smoke, even as the oil starts to burn itself out. It seems to get more and more intense in fact, as the flames die. And the wind seems to be against them, blowing it into the darkness. The vampires grab Arianna and move back further into the cave. There is no way out for them. But they can't imagine that the shepherds would come so far into the cave. And there is nothing about the smoke that is deadly for them. It's just very uncomfortable. The cave is fortunately too damp for it to burn anything significant.

All the vampires need to do is pass the time until the sun sets again. There is just the small matter of the smoke and the fact that they are stuck in the back of a cave. So breathing is going to be a little uncomfortable for at least twelve hours. But then they will show the ambitious seven just what it is that they have set themselves up for.

Arianna knows that Tanner is no longer in the cave with her. Her senses too are returning. It's the awareness that the love that she feels seems to have been severed. It is not something that she expected. But she is overcome by the feeling that maybe he has actually managed to get away. She knows that Luke was here, remembering his smell from the last time they were together. There is just no way that she can be sure though, her own hunger getting her to the point where her consciousness feels like a dream.

Credo looks like he has been satisfied sexually. This is because he has. The others sense that there has been some serious fucking in their absence. Karl places a finger inside Arianna, not too concerned for the seven outside anymore, confident in their ability come night. For now, they have a few hours to play with Arianna so they may as well enjoy it. The Leadership isn't expecting them until nightfall anyway.

The intensity of the standoff outside grows. The wolves are getting less anxious as the clouds start to roll in again. The rain is coming back. And it looks like it is coming back worse than it's been. This is really not looking as good for them as it was a minute ago. But at least Tanner seems to be getting some of his fight back; he too is on his feet. They have no choice but to use some more of their oil to keep their torches burning. But when the rain starts falling, there will be no hope.

The wolves retreat onto nearby rocks to wait for their meal. It shouldn't be long now, a light drizzle already starting to fall. The torches are not going to last very long. And then it's going to be tickets for Tanner and his rescuers. But the shepherds aren't just about keeping them at bay. They have some skills learned from their training sabbatical. They also have some decent daggers stuck to the end of their staff.

The odds are even. The shepherds go in for the attack. The wolves aren't sure if they want to tire them out or go in for the kill. They are not sure if they want to risk the fire but the shepherds are really taunting them, playing on their egos so that the wolves engage. The fight takes on a very quick momentum and wolves start to fall. Tanner isn't strong enough to be any good in the fight so he focuses on the fire.

The training has paid off and soon the wolves that haven't been killed are heading for the hills. They know that the dogs will be getting reinforcements. Tanner is at the mouth of the cave and Luke calls for him to come back. But Tanner is determined to get to Arianna. He throws more oil on the entrance and lights it. The cave fills with more and more smoke.

The shepherds watch in horror as Tanner goes into the cave, no warning and no turning back. His determination to get to her pisses Luke off. But he can't bring himself to follow his brother into the cave. He just hates that this vampire woman seems to have got her claws into him. He wants her dead. There is no way that he can get to her to finish her, though, and now his brother has made all their efforts a futile exercise as he goes right back into the prison they've just freed him from.

Tanner gets very close to the back of the cave. The vampires can't make out his scent from all the smoke. He can see that Arianna is still naked and that she is also quickly being overwhelmed by the smoke. He needs to get to her. And he needs to get to her quickly. Fortunately, the vampires are starting to risk moving toward the mouth of the cave, just for the little bit of fresh air that they can get there.

There is no time to waste. Tanner gets flat on the ground and crawls slowly to Arianna. He reaches her after what feels like forever.

"Arianna?" He speaks her name into her ear. She just coughs. Tanner cuts into himself and places it over her mouth. She takes a deep breath and then grabs his arm, biting into it. She sucks hard and Tanner screams before he can stop himself.

As Arianna feeds Tanner can hear the vampires moving toward them. They move slowly, the bulk of the smoke now on the inside of the cave. But the smell of Tanner's blood draws them like the moon. By the time they get to them, there is no denying that Tanner has provided Arianna with just enough of what she needs.

She jumps to her feet as Tanner slumps to the ground. Even though she is a little shaky, she is in fine form. She takes to the vampires aggressively and rips their heads from their bodies. Her favorite to get to is Credo. Then she remembers Karl. But when she searches for him, he is nowhere to be seen. She wants him. She needs to get her hands on his head...

CHAPTER 10

THE SMOKE IS in her eyes now and filling her lungs. Tanner too is dealing with her bite and the lack of oxygen in the cave. Arianna is trying hard to sense Karl, who she knows could not have left the cave. But the smoke has both vampires confused. Karl knows that he just needs to avoid Arianna, and attack her when he has the element of surprise. He knows that she too cannot leave the cave, not just yet.

As she drags herself toward the fresh air at the mouth of the cave for Tanner's sake mostly, she doesn't realize that she has left Karl in the back of the cave. He too is facedown in the mud. The Cave is filling fast with water as the rain comes down outside. It's still no more than a drizzle but it's excessive. The little bit of sunshine that allowed for Tanner's rescue is gone as quickly as it appeared. Karl watches as Arianna struggles to get Tanner to the mouth of the cave. But he is turning quite fast and he is putting up a struggle of his own.

"It's going to be alright Tanner...you're going to be alright." She says this to try to get him to work with her. But her words fall on deaf ears. Tanner doesn't know what is happening to him or where he is. There is just an intense pain and confusion coursing through his veins. "You really shouldn't have done that...that was such a stupid thing to do..." She looks to where his hand is still bleeding from her bite.

They get to the mouth and it's easier to breathe. But there is no way for Arianna to get any further. It's still daylight. She also doesn't have the strength yet to toss Tanner to safety. Then she realizes that he is as safe as he can be inside with her. She looks at his arm again, watches as he writhes on the ground, and remembers that now he is not too far from becoming like her. Suddenly she hates herself. But she knows that she didn't do this intentionally. In fact, until after she bit him, she had no idea who it was that she was biting into. But it's too late to cry over spilled blood.

The sounds from outside, the rain against the rocks, reminds her suddenly of her entire ordeal. Anger builds up inside her. She can think of more than one vampire that she could kill; a couple of wolves too. But she isn't ready. She isn't strong enough yet to handle a full-on battle. And she knows that the only reason that she managed to beat these vampires here now was because of her diet. This diet gives her a bit of an edge over them. But at the moment it isn't much of an edge.

Then she hears the shepherds outside. They have a new set of wolves in the clearing. This group didn't just stumble upon them. They've been making their way through the forest hoping for a taste of Arianna who they had been told was inside. But instead of waiting for the pussy, they find a mangle of dead wolves and seven humans with nothing but staffs and torches about to go out in the rain. But there is a brighter fire burning in the young men's eyes and the wolves know that they are in for quite a fight.

"Just how many of you dogs are there?" Luke screams through the rain at the wolves.

"More than you will ever be able to manage..." One of the wolves speaks loudly, growling and salivating.

The wolves can sense Arianna. She also has a strong sense of them. They lust for her and are even more irritated by the inconvenience that the shepherds represent. But it shouldn't be too much of an effort. The shepherds look like they have already had more than they can take. But still, there is a fire burning in their eyes.

The wolves go in. And the shepherds steel themselves. More oil is needed on their lamps and they are anxious about this. But there is no choice. If their light goes out, the wolves will be deterred by nothing. So they light up and the torches become incredible orbs for a second and then become decent flames. The wolves move back a little and try to find an in. The shepherds don't wait for the wolves to make a move. They go for them.

Arianna tunes in to the battle, impressed by the fight with the shepherds. The wolves drop fast again despite the exhaustion of the humans, and finally, the last dogs left standing retreat back into the forest.

"This isn't over, you'll be sorry..." The wolves growl as they disappear, promising all sorts of revenge.

"Bring it on you vermin..." The shepherds are undeterred.

The shepherds look around wildly now, not because of the wolves, their fire, and the rain, but because the sun is going down. They hadn't realized just how long they had been fighting already. As soon as the sun sets the vampires will come in droves. The vampires will be more than a little angry. And they have no deterrent for the vampires. It will be hand-to-hand combat. It will all come down to their training. There is no secret weapon save that they know that the head must be removed from the body completely...

Inside the cave, Arianna hears the faintest movement in the darkness behind her. She throws her eyes outside and deduces that it is still too risky to exit. She senses that there could be another fight looming. She knows that it is Karl in the cave with her. And she knows that he will not go down without putting up one hell of a fight. Arianna takes a deep breath and tries to get a measure of her strength. She's not feeling too worse for wear, but her movements are still a little bit shaky.

Karl can sense that the day is coming to an end. Soon enough Arianna will make her exit with Tanner, whose humanness will soon be no more. There will then be two vampires for Karl to fight. He remembers the sound of Arianna feeding on Tanner, and how she killed the others. This isn't something he really wants to risk. And he also doesn't want to be left with his tail between his legs when the Leadership wants an explanation as to why they managed to capture her but did not manage to hold on to her.

If she gets away now, after all the effort to capture her, this will make the Leadership very unhappy. They will have to explain, or at least Karl will have to explain why they didn't just bring her straight to them. Of course, they know why, and would themselves have done exactly the same thing if there were a reversal of roles. But still, Karl hates that he will have to report this, fearing for his life if they deemed him incompetent.

Karl knows what he needs to do and he starts to edge forward toward Arianna and Tanner. Tanner is recoiling now madly, rolling wildly on the floor. He looks every bit like a pig in mud. Karl knows that it could be a little while yet before Tanner becomes a vampire, and even then he will be easy to kill. It takes new vampires a minute to figure things out. Arianna is the one he needs to focus on first, the one he can't let get away. He must fight her...kill her...Karl must be the one to deliver her final blow.

Even without the body, which will disappear, the leadership will smell her death on Karl's hands. When one vampire kills another, they are stained, like gunshot residue. It's not visible for long. But the smell lingers. The smell lingers for a very long time. So Karl will have his evidence that he is the one who carried out the deed. His hands will carry the confirmation of Arianna's death.

Tanner has stopped shaking now. Arianna hopes that he is dead but knows that he isn't. However, the stillness is strange and eerie. She puts her face close to his, wanting some sign of how far along he is exactly in the process.

"Tanner?" She speaks into his ear. He doesn't respond so she doesn't know if he has even heard her. "Tanner, are you okay?" She has asked the question before realizing its absurdity. Still, there is no movement from Tanner. She takes him in her arms and for a moment forgets everything around them, everything that has just happened to them, and she just holds the man she knows now has given up his life for her. Tanner can't possibly know what his new existence will entail. But it will certainly be no life.

Karl is close enough now to them to see that this is his moment. He gets to Arianna just as she realizes his presence and takes a firm hold of her ankle. He lifts off the ground and pulls a naked Arianna through the mud before lifting her off the ground just a little. She lets go completely of Tanner, not wanting to drag him with her. She should have just forced him out of the cave. He would have been dead by now. She doesn't want Tanner to have to deal with anything else after everything that he has already had to deal with for her sake.

Both Arianna and Karl hiss violently. So violently that they are heard outside the cave and the shepherds can't help but glare into the darkness, wondering. "You do know that it didn't have to be like this Arianna. You could have just accepted the gift you were given and live out your life as a vampire, with other vampires…" Karl has such a firm grip on her that it feels as if her bones might snap. Arianna doesn't justify his sentiments with an answer.

All she can think of is that Tanner must be killed before he turns completely. This has been decided this already. But with the firm grip on her ankle, and Karl's awareness that she isn't herself, there is no way for her to get to him to finish him off. She is really going to have to try her best to make this fight quick. Tanner doesn't deserve the life that her bite has now condemned him to. Nobody deserves this life.

She turns herself so that she is looking up at Karl and then she pushes up. She pushes with all that she is worth so that Karl is pressed between her and the roof of the cave. He is caught by surprise by how strong she seems to be suddenly. This is probably a result of her attention to her intention, which is of course to get Tanner out safely; or so Karl thinks. Arianna pulls down a little and then flips them over before plunging Karl into the mud with a splash. Karl pushes back.

"You will not get out of here alive, accept that. And neither will your boyfriend." Karl speaks up from the mud as he tries to lift Arianna off himself. The way he says 'boyfriend' pisses Arianna off and she pushes down harder, hoping that there is enough soft earth under Karl for her to be able to submerge him in the brown muck. But there isn't, and Karl is not a weak vampire. He digs into his reserves and pushes up so hard that he sends Arianna into the roof of the cave with a loud thud that brings some of the looser rocks down with her.

Karl grabs a hold of her as soon as she has landed in the mud next to him and then rolls on top of her. Her nakedness is distracting but also gives Karl an idea of how to make this fight easier. She is exposed to him in every possible way. All the parts that he will need to distract her just enough to kill her are wide open. And he knows that she knows what he felt like inside her. All he needs to do is nudge her imagination in the right direction.

Arianna's strength is being restored in waves. She has sudden bursts of super strength and then feels a little shaky. She pulls Karl to her, closer, and wraps her arms around him. He struggles, but she rolls with it, and again she has Karl in the mud. He struggles some more to get her off him but fails. Arianna is as formidable an opponent as she's ever been.

Karl takes a muddy hand between her legs and runs his cold fingers along the surface of Arianna's clit. She shudders at his touch and he takes advantage of this distraction that lasts only seconds. In a flash, it is Karl who is on top of Arianna again. He knows his real power is his way with a woman. And he knows that Arianna isn't immune to his touch. So he will fight this battle with his strongest weapon.

"Feels like it needs to be visited again, don't you think?" He speaks while rubbing his fingers harder over her pussy.

"Not by you, you beast!" She sounds more convincing in her heart. This amuses Karl. He can't help himself from laughing.

Then he puts his lips on hers and by the time she realizes it he already has his tongue inside her mouth. He can't be serious. He can't actually be kissing her. But he is. And Arianna's body is responding as it should to Karl's expert touch. Then his tongue is out and he is rubbing his lips against hers. She can't breathe as he sends tremors through her. Karl lifts off her to observe his handy work.

Arianna comes round and pushes Karl off of her and the away. She hates that she can't hide her bulging clit and perked-up breasts. Karl's touch has triggered all her responses and now she looks ready to fuck. But this is just a tactic she knows. He is distracting her from the fight so that he can kill her. And at the rate he is going, it won't be long before he does if she doesn't pull herself together.

Tanner lets out a scream and both Karl and Arianna look over in his direction. This one doesn't sound like anything they've heard before. And both of them have witnessed a fair amount of turnings. This worries Karl because he isn't sure what type of vampire Tanner is going to become. And he knows that it's going to be a mission enough just to deal with Arianna. The thought of a hybrid Tanner is one that doesn't sit well with him. Karl suddenly feels the pressure to deal swiftly with Arianna so that if he has to face Tanner, it will be Tanner alone that he has to face.

Because of her feelings for him, Arianna is more distracted by Tanner's pain than Karl is. This is the gap that he needs. And again he has Arianna pinned down in the mud. Arianna looks to where Tanner is, trying to get a sense of where he is in his turning. Karl in the meantime sticks his finger so deep into her that she tenses around it with every muscle inside of her pussy. Her legs shake and she has to tense them too just to get over the feeling that she was falling off the edge of the world.

Karl keeps his finger where it is and then moves it around in circles. Despite her hissing Arianna is also fed his tongue. Karl kisses her with the same aggression with which he is fingering her. He goes at her hard with his fingers, needing to weaken her defenses just enough for him to be able to get his hands on her neck. Also, he can't help but get as much of a taste of Arianna as he can before he kills her.

She can't help her vaginal response to the finger inside it. Karl takes advantage of this and adds a second finger. He uses all his upper body strength to hold Arianna down as he moves his fingers around inside her moistening vagina which is surrendering long before the rest of her body. She hates this feeling of vulnerability and the fact that again Karl has her where he wants her.

He too is aroused now as he digs around inside her. But not too aroused as to forget how this has to end. He rubs his erection against her leg and breathes into her face as he continues to weaken her with the muddy fingers in her wetness. Arianna tries to push up out of the mud but her efforts are in vain. Karl is very good at what he does.

"This is no doubt some of the best pussy on the planet, you know that. Such a pity that it has to go up in flames. You really didn't live out your true purpose Arianna. You really didn't make full use of your real skill. Your real power is right here. This is where your true strength has always been." Karl says this while going harder into Arianna so that she knows exactly what parts of her he is referring to. She loses just a little of her fight as she allows herself to be reduced to the wonders of her cunt.

But then Arianna remembers Tanner and tries harder to pull herself from the erotic lull Karl is pushing her toward.

She needs to be strong for him, after the sacrifices that he has already made for her. She can't give up on him, on them. Then Tanner moans so loudly that the cave seems to vibrate. More rocks fall on them from above. Karl looks over to see what is happening with him. Arianna moves her hand onto his bulge at this moment and Karl's erection fills completely. He is taken aback.

"If you want to play, let's play. But this time, I suggest you don't hold back!" Arianna gives Karl's cock a firm squeeze and then uses her nails to rip an opening in his pants large enough to bring the meat out into the open. She runs up and down the shaft with the lightest fingers and then squeezes the hardness again. Karl looks at her and isn't sure what the challenge is that Arianna is presenting to him.

Then Arianna moves her knee up between Karl's legs. She kicks him so hard that he lifts far enough off of her for his fingers to make a swift exit from her vagina. Arianna lifts herself out of the mud and then takes hold of Karl with both hands. She continues to lift up toward the top of the cave but the smoke seems to have lifted and lingered there and she and Karl both start to cough. Arianna takes her hands to Karl's head as she makes her way back down toward the muddy floor but she can't get a grip.

Outside Luke and his friends are becoming increasingly concerned for themselves now as the rain starts to come down a little harder. There is the definite possibility that their lamps will go out, the only protection they have against the wolves. Then there will be a full-contact battle that they might not survive. They look into the cave but can't really see anything. The cave goes completely black just beyond the mouth. Luke wonders if his brother is even still alive. The shepherds also know that now that night is upon them, the vampires will be back. But not once does it cross their minds to leave without Tanner.

"I can't leave him...dead or alive I just won't leave him. I want to be the one to bury him...if it has come to that." Luke is speaking to himself really but the others have heard him and share his sentiments. Nobody is going anywhere.

Inside, Arianna brings herself to standing. Karl grabs a hold of her thighs as she tries to rub some of the mud off her body. It doesn't work. Frustrated, she runs her hands through her hair, which is also muddy. But it helps and her hands are a little less slippery. She grabs hold of Karl's head and pulls hard. But it doesn't snap. Instead, Karl is standing up in front of her suddenly so that she has to let go of his head because he is so tall.

"You will not leave this cave alive Arianna. I promise you that." Karl himself now is less convinced of what he is saying, not sure where Arianna is getting so much fight from. Every time he thinks he has her, she comes back harder. And she's come too close too often now to snapping his neck.

Karl takes his fingers into her hair. He battles to get a grip but still manages to pull hard enough to give Arianna an instant headache. She grabs her own hair and pulls it back from between her attacker's thick fingers. But no sooner has she freed herself and Karl is back on her, gripping her around her neck with his fingers and squeezing hard. Arianna struggles to free herself now as she senses the very real possibility of her neck snapping.

Tanner comes to her rescue again. In his state, he lets out another scream and starts to say something that nobody can understand. It's a deeply guttural muttering that Arianna can't recall hearing since the beginning of her vampire existence. Karl too can't remember a turning being quite so dramatic. And he has done his fair share of turnings. There is something different about Tanner that makes Karl very, very uneasy.

Arianna takes the opportunity that has been presented to her. Instead of trying to hold on to Karl's head, she grabs his hair and gives him a taste of his own medicine, pulling back and then down in a quick movement. For the briefest moment, Karl's head seems to snap back forward and so Arianna gives it another solid yank in the opposite direction so that the tear along his throat is a perfect red line. Arianna holds his head in her hands now and twists it off completely.

It's over for Karl, and he is the one who won't be leaving the cave alive. He incinerates and vanishes in a gray powder, disappearing into the mud. Arianna has so much adrenalin pumping through her that she still looks around the cave, almost expecting to see Karl. But then she sees Tanner and makes her way to him, realizing that she has done it. She has killed Karl. Looking at Tanner though, and remembering what she has done to him, the kill isn't as satisfying as she had hoped.

Arianna wraps herself around Tanner as he convulses. She isn't sure how far he is from being a vampire, his turning taking longer than she's seen any turning take. And one thing is definitely clear. Tanner is in incredible pain. Arianna wants to end this pain. She just wants to snap his head off his neck and have him rest in peace. But she remembers his brother who came all this way to save him. Luke deserves some say in this, and she needs to give him an opportunity to say goodbye to Tanner if he wants to.

She keeps him close and tries to talk him into calming down. It doesn't help. All that happens is that his seizures get progressively worse. She holds on tighter. Both of them are now shuddering as Arianna tries to contain the situation. Eventually, she accepts that there is nothing that she can do but hold him until he is done turning. But then Tanner passes out completely and is almost lifeless save for the faintest heartbeat.

The darkness outside fuses with the darkness in the cave now and Arianna knows that it's night. She goes over to the entrance of the cave, Tanner over her shoulders. He is remarkably heavy now, even for her. There is no time to wonder too much about the reception she is going to get from the seven men outside. But she needs to get out of the cave. It's been too much too long. She needs to also get to the shepherds and figure out what to do because there is bound to be a battalion on its way to them.

Luke is the first to spot the shadow exiting the cave. As Arianna comes into focus he can see that she is carrying Tanner.

"Is he dead?" Luke asks the question loud enough for the others to look in Arianna's direction. "Is he dead?" He screams the question at Arianna now.

She doesn't know how to answer him. All she does is put Tanner down on the ground and hope that the question will answer itself soon enough. But Tanner doesn't move, and to all watching, he looks dead. Arianna knows that he isn't. As faint as it is, she can hear his heartbeat. But she can also hear something else. They need to get away from here. She lifts Tanner over her shoulders again, realizing as she raises him over her head that she is still naked.

"We've got to get away from here." It's obvious in her voice that she is completely exhausted. But she tries for a commanding tone.

"Is my brother dead?" Luke isn't going to move until he knows. The others watch as it seems like things are going to heat up for all the wrong reasons between Arianna and Luke.

"He won't be alive for very long, and neither will the rest of us, if we don't get as far away from her as possible, now! They look from her to each other and then pick up their staffs, following Arianna into the forest, but only because she is carrying one of their own.

Tanner lets out a scream and then jerks so violently that he throws Arianna to the ground. The shepherds see the marks on his arm and know that something is very wrong. Arianna says nothing, just lifting Tanner up again as soon as his seizure stops. They know that he has been bitten and that he is becoming one of them. Despite their renewed anger toward the undead, they still follow Arianna through the woods.

CHAPTER 11

THE FOREST FLOOR IS WET. And the darkness makes it even more difficult to navigate. Luke would like to be the one holding his brother but this makes no sense, given that Tanner is really almost all vampire now. Arianna wants to kill him, to end it before it's too late. But she needs to get Luke and the others as far from here as possible, to safety.

It's almost midnight when they get to a safe place, deep in the forest. Arianna places Tanner on the ground and Luke makes a dash for him. But Arianna warns them all against this.

"That's not a very good idea..." She says, completely oblivious to her nakedness now.

"It wasn't a good idea for you to bite him in the first place..." Luke is livid.

"I had no choice...He forced me..." Arianna has a very weak defense...

"You always have a choice. We all always have a bloody choice..." Luke's passion seems almost exaggerated.

Luke lifts a large stump and moves menacingly toward Arianna. The others aren't sure whether to pull him back or to leave him, knowing how fiercely Luke has always loved Tanner. It takes them a minute to realize that perhaps killing Arianna wouldn't be the best thing. She is the only one who can save them from Tanner once he's turned if he has no idea who they are.

Arianna understands Luke's fury and will try not to fight back if he indeed came at her, even though it is quite clear that he wants to kill her. And with the way they fought off the wolves, it's clear that they've really gone out of their way to develop their skills. They could do some serious damage. Then Tanner lets out a type of scream that Arianna knows only too well. His turning is almost complete.

"We have to kill him before he becomes like them...like me...we can't let him become like me..." She is pleading with Luke.

It's clear that Luke doesn't want to lose his brother. But Tanner is lost to him either way. And the thought of adding another vampire to the world is one that doesn't sit very well with any of the shepherds.

"I'll do it. I'll be the one to end my brother's life..." Luke sounds about as convincing as he can. But the thought of killing Tanner makes his stomach turn. They have the skills. They have the weapons. But Luke would no sooner kill Arianna and take his chances with his big brother.

The war of words goes on a little too long and by the time everyone looks at Tanner again, he is on his feet, looking around wildly. Everyone, even Arianna, moves back, giving him the space to figure out this new animal that he's become. Tanner looks directly at Luke, holding his gaze. He salivates like a werewolf but doesn't charge. Arianna readies herself for anything, as do the others.

Nobody moves as Tanner gets uncomfortably close to

Luke. Luke moves toward him, slowly, surprising himself and everyone else. This could go very, very badly indeed. But still, the brothers move toward one another. Arianna wants to speak but knows that this might set Tanner off. She can only watch now, to see how much of his former self was lost during the turning.

The brothers are close enough now for them to breathe into each other's faces. Luke isn't scared. This is his brother. And nothing that Tanner can do to him now will change the way he feels. He knows that whatever Tanner does now would definitely not be of his own doing. For a split second Luke throws an icy stare at Arianna, the orchestrator of this monumental disaster.

"Brother..." Tanner's voice is his but not. He looks straight into Luke's eyes, almost blinding him with a series of glows that are completely unnatural.

"Tanner...Tanner...You're still you?!" Luke throws his arms around his brother. Incredible pulses move through Tanner's body and Luke actually can't hold on. He releases his brother from his embrace but holds his gaze.

"Thank you brother...thank you...Luke..." A smile comes over Tanner's face when he says his brother's name, and a tear falls down his face.

But then Tanner is on the ground, rolling around, convulsing, and hissing such a hideous hiss that everyone, even Luke, creates as much distance between themselves and him as they possibly can. He sounds like every serpent in hell come to earth. Arianna takes a firm hold of him and lifts them both up in the air. She speaks into his ear words that nobody can hear but Tanner.

"I'm sorry...I should never have done this to you..." She too has tears rolling down her face.

Tanner can't respond. He has no idea where he is or

what is going on with him again. All he knows is that it hurts like hell. His head fills with memories that seem to belong to someone else. And no matter how hard he tries, nothing seems to belong to him anymore. Arianna gets them back on solid ground and the pair lies naked on the earth, side by side, Arianna holding on to Tanner while he seems to have a series of intense seizures. She can't bring herself to tell him that it's going to be okay. She knows that nothing can be okay now.

Then calm settles over Tanner as he loses himself to his new state. He opens his eyes and sees seven faces, familiar but not, staring back at him in the darkness. He searches for one, finds it. There is a familiarity in his gaze that calms Luke almost immediately. Arianna moves in closer to Tanner, aware of her nakedness fully for the first time and so trying to hide it. Tanner too realizes that not only is he naked, but he is also starting to grow one mother of a boner.

Luke and his friends look around for somewhere they can rest, and also give the pair the privacy they're obviously going to need now. Tanner looks at Arianna, who is watching the others disappear into the darkness. Her skin is tingling to the point where she appears, at least to Tanner, to be glowing in the dark. He too is tingling through parts of him he wasn't aware had any sensation. He looks to where his dick is throbbing between his legs, his erection a powerful pulsing mass.

He looks at Arianna, seeing her almost clearly for the first time. The dark seems to enhance his ability to really see things now. The giddiness subsides and Tanner feels more of a man than he has been in his entire existence. The entire world now seems possible for him. Arianna now seems possible for him. And here she is, naked in his arms, tingling alongside him, with him, wanting him.

"I have wanted you for a very long time, Arianna..." Tanner knows himself from before. He knows what he has wanted.

"I've yearned for you, too, Tanner, since I left you at the hospital. But not like this. I wanted you...Now because of me you are this. Now you are them..." It settles over Arianna that her dream of being loved by a normal man will never come true now. She realizes that because of her, the man she wants to be with is no longer normal.

"I gave you what you needed Arianna...You were going to die. This isn't your fault. It's mine. And I'm still me. I just get to be me now with you forever...forever." Tanner speaks as though he has an understanding of what forever means. He doesn't.

The forest around them stills now, and both Arianna and Tanner can hear, too clearly, that the seven have already fallen fast asleep. They don't blame them. Fuck it's been an intense time. But now the intensity is centered on two vampires who have been able only to make love to each other in their imaginations. And the tension has built up to the point where even Arianna and Tanner are afraid of what is going to go down now in the real world.

Tanner listens out for in the silence, and senses in a way he can't yet explain that there's a den a few feet from them, hollowed out of the base of a rock. He moves Arianna to it and is pleased that it can comfortably accommodate them both. It's probably the hibernation chamber of a large bear, or two. And if the beast comes back, Tanner is confident in his competence to send it packing.

He feels like he can't breathe. Arianna feels the same. They are locked in an embrace that has more to do with how they feel than what they feel. The tremors moving through them from each other have the pair shuddering.

The leafy foliage that is their bed is warm and intriguingly cool, the sweat from the two undead strange and warm. Tanner centers himself as he accepts that he is now Arianna's equal, sort of. He has confidence that he couldn't muster even in his dreams that he will be able to please Arianna in every possible way.

Their faces are close, their breaths fusing. Tanner cannot hold back from placing his lips on Arianna's any longer, and their mouths meet. Sparks fly into the other's mouth from the other. It is everything that it had been in his head. Arianna's too. Despite the shuddering, they don't shudder away from each other, but into one another, Tanner's tongue deep inside Arianna's mouth.

She is on her back and Tanner is on top of her, trying not to settle on top of her with his full weight. Then he lifts off her completely, unintentionally, and hovers just above her, the weight of his dick forming a diagonal so that its tip rests on Arianna's belly. She reaches for it and strokes it lightly as Tanner processes his ability to lift himself off the ground and into the air.

Arianna continues to move her hands along the penis that is everything it was in her dreams and then some. Tanner continues to shake. He also continues to lift higher and higher off Arianna until she has to reach for him. But the den they are in is designed by an animal for lying down. And so Tanner's flight of fancy comes to an abrupt end when he reaches the roof.

With herself lifting off now too Arianna reaches Tanner quickly. She parts her legs and settles him between them. Then she wraps around him and eases them both back onto the soft earth. The space is now warmer thanks to their body heat and their breathing and Arianna is completely relaxed, loving the associations of comfort, warmth, and safety. Also, since she had spent a large part of the last while being the star of a very elaborate exhibition in vampire and wolf sexual prowess, that she is now alone with the man of her dreams is almost beyond belief. She has a new appreciation for privacy.

There are a million games that the couple can play. There are as many things that they would like to do to each other forever. But since forever is something they now have, they move swiftly to the one thing that will take all their desires and tie them in a perfect knot. It's time for Tanner and Arianna to make their collective dreams come true.

He wraps around her so forcefully that she has to give back equal resistance to avoid being crushed. Tanner hasn't comprehended his new strength. He feels her resistance and looks into her eyes, questioning. She is quick to reassure him that it has nothing to do with stopping the proceedings, and everything to do with making sure that they continue. He laughs at himself and loosens his hold a little. Arianna relaxes as well.

Then Tanner's reinvigorated power tool settles on Arianna's pussy and starts to find its way inside her. Tanner wants to kiss her while this happens but he can hardly breathe. So he just concentrates on gently moving his erection into the Promised Land, and enjoying the look on Arianna's face and the sounds escaping her mouth as he fills her completely with his love.

She is now the one who is gripping him tightly so that Tanner counters her hold. They both laugh, Tanner pulling his dick from her as slowly as he inserted it. Then he moves it back into her and finds the fiery rear cove of her vagina. It is hotter than he had made it in his head. And it seems to have the life that makes him think there is a bevy of staff inside Arianna's pussy whose job it is to service his tool.

It's not human what Arianna's pussy is managing on his dick and Tanner realizes that he is going to need a measure of focus before he is settled enough to totally lose himself in her. He gathers his thoughts and tries to link them to his emotions. But still, the physical overwhelms. Arianna holds Tanner to her tightly and encourages him to just breathe.

He does and pulls part of himself from inside her. Then he breathes again and moves back into her. Arianna just breathes and receives him. Tanner gets himself positioned while Arianna holds him there. They give each other just enough room to move. Tanner keeps going in and out of Arianna until, finally, he gets into a rhythm.

His power seems to have increased now with his confidence. Tanner suddenly knows what he is doing and also what he is capable of. Arianna can feel this too and so she relinquishes more and more control of herself to him. It's time. She can feel it. The time has finally come where Tanner is going to actually make full and total love to her. Every muscle melts. Every part of her softens. Every part of Arianna now belongs to Tanner to do with as he pleases.

And he pleases. Over and over again, Tanner does to Arianna all the things he had dreamed and by default all the things that she had. They are saying nothing to each other but yet both of them are doing everything that the other has in mind. They can literally read each other's minds. And they answer each other with their bodies. The den warms rapidly and soon enough it is the warmest love nest, the safest of cocoons.

They make love with no concern for the outside world. Neither of them knows if the sun has come or gone. They are consumed with one another. Even the seven outside are now forgotten. The seven though are still aware of their situation and sleep in turns as they listen, while trying not to, at the lovemaking that is so intense the earth literally does shake. All seven are a little jealous of the new Tanner.

As Tanner continues to move in and out of Arianna, as he slides up and down on top of her, the earth under Arianna gives way. Before long they have fucked a trench into the dirt that makes the den even bigger. It's a good thing too, because the more comfortable Tanner is with himself, the more adventurous and experimental he becomes with Arianna. Now they start to explore the other things they wanted to do with one another, to one another, in the beginning.

They face each other on their sides, looking deep into one another's eyes, kissing, giggling, speaking, and not speaking. Tanner is careful about losing the connection and positions himself a little deeper inside Arianna just to be sure. Then he continues to kiss her, rolling her over several times as he does, deepening the trench.

Then he manages to have her on her belly, his arms wrapped around her so that her nipples don't touch the ground. He goes into her from behind but still manages to fill her completely with himself. Tanner rests his face on Arianna's back and their sweats mix. Then he uses his forehead to clear the wetness enough for him to kiss her back as he handles her womanhood.

Arianna cannot believe just how right Tanner gets it, over and over again. He just gets into every part of her and makes it all a million times better than it was. Over and over Tanner confirms everything that Arianna had ever dared to hope about him. When he turns her back onto her backside so that he is on top of her and inside her and able to kiss her and look into her eyes, her heart melts into his and she closes her eyes, trusting Tanner now completely with herself.

For as long as they need time and space, Luke and the others give it to them. What seems like forever to Tanner and Arianna has actually just been a couple of hours. And the sun is now coming up so the pair needs to stay put. Luke and his mates find food, clean up in a nearby river, and start to make plans for the journey home. Then they get some more rest, waiting for the sunset again so that they can find out from Tanner and Arianna what they intend doing from here.

Everyone is a little uncomfortable though that they haven't seen a hair from the vampire or the wolf. It's strange that these beasts that vowed revenge have made no attempt to find them...

CHAPTER 12

THERE IS a carefreeness about the way the young woman takes her clothes off and walks into the tiny pond. She doesn't even look around to see if anyone is watching her. The peeping toms who usually do seem to be mastering their craft now, she can hear nothing but the natural sounds around her. She disappears under the water to escape the late afternoon heat and wash off her day's work.

She wouldn't usually be alone, her fellow milkmaids also fond of the cool water after a long day's work. But she is the only one today. This probably explains the quietness around her. Maybe the young men like the vision of many maidens naked in the pond. But this has been a particularly hard day and all the other girls want to do is go home and rest up before making supper for their families.

Being completely submerged in the water has the effect of making the beautiful woman feel like she has disappeared into another world that belongs to nobody but herself. If only she could stay beneath the surface forever. Even the pain from her many recent losses seems to disappear as she drops herself far beneath the surface and lingers naively between the underwater foliage. But soon she is swimming in the dark, and she knows it's time to get home.

The sounds of night take over the atmosphere before the sun has even set completely. It's easy not to feel unsafe in the beauty of the sunset and the normalcy of the day becoming a beautiful evening. But the world isn't what it used to be. And to pretend that it proves very often to be a very deadly mistake. Many have fallen because of naivety and ignorance. But tonight seems to be one of those nights where dismissing fear and anxiety comes easily. She's always been told by her brothers that to live in fear is no way to live. So she exits the water as though nobody could possibly be watching.

But she is being watched, by expert watchers. The wolves have managed to make themselves inconspicuous and silent. Fia continues to move out of the cool water, unaware that she is being watched, but very aware that her mother will want her back soon. She walks slowly out of the pond, enjoying the feeling of the mud between her toes. She would give anything to go back under and stay there for as long as she can hold her breath. She wishes that she could become a fish and stay under there where evil has no power. But life is what it is.

On dry land, she shakes the water off of herself and then squeezes it out of her hair. Her perfect breasts take in the last of the light. She moves her hands over herself so that she can move more water off herself before she puts on her clothes. Her hand lingers briefly as it always does between her legs and then she catches herself, checking her surrounds out of habit. She really enjoys touching herself. She hasn't been ready to let herself be touched by a man like this, not wanting to deal with the reality of sex just yet.

All her friends have told her that it isn't the way you grow up imagining it in your head.

Fia is suddenly aware of movement and hurries to cover herself up. No sooner has she covered up when she is surrounded by four wolves. She looks around beyond the dogs and sees nothing. She wonders for a second at how she could have been so careless, how even after all the training and warnings from her brothers, how she could have let her guard down so completely. But then she reminds herself about not living in fear, even with what happened to her friends, one of whom was her brother's girlfriend.

She really is much like her brothers, despite her delicate and fragile appearance. Fia is hardened to the beasts that have turned their world into a living nightmare. She looks from one to the other, making sure to pull her dress up completely so that the wolves see no more of her nakedness deliberately. Whatever they want from her now they will have to take. And she will not let it go without a fight. She knows that it is a fight she can never win. But she owes it to all the training her brothers forced on her to die fighting.

Tanner and Luke have taught their sister well. She doesn't scream. She doesn't even acknowledge the wolves really, knowing that whatever happens now, she can do nothing about how it will end. She knows that screaming will bring people to her who will probably also just end up dead. This isn't necessary. The wolves round her repeatedly, salivating. So it's clear that they want her. There is no need for anyone else to get hurt.

"You're not afraid?" one of the wolves asks eventually, taken aback by how she isn't anxious in any way.

"Of what, you... Don't be stupid. Do what you've come to do and be done with it." Fia stands taller as she speaks to make clear her resolve.

The wolves almost don't know what to make of this beauty that they've been sent to kidnap. The vampires are no longer taking things for granted and so they want collateral that will bring Arianna and Tanner to them; and how better to do that than to take the one thing that Tanner and Luke love more than life itself. The wolves take hold of Fia and disappear with her into the night.

With her mouth gagged and her hands and legs bound, the wolves stop occasionally to wreak havoc on the villages they pass. Fia knows that it's strange that they are not already taking advantage of her, devouring her delicate punani the way they are doing to the others they come across. Why would they simply be taking her away? Where to? It seems so pointless because she is too tiny to survive for any length of time once they start to take to her with their dicks. It seems such an extravagant waste of time. But she won't wonder at or entertain the thinking of these things.

They have their fill of the locals on the way to the forest and then carry Fia into the dark woods. She makes her own peace with her impending end and this calms her quickly. Already she has said her goodbyes to her loved ones in her heart, especially her mother. They have all believed for a while that her brothers have long since been lost. Fia doesn't mind dying. She will be as brave in death as her brothers had always been in life.

Her head starts to spin as they move faster and faster. She knows from their conversation that they are afraid of whoever it is they are going to. She gathers that she is being taken to something even worse than the wolves. Fia wonders why but then doesn't spend too much time trying to figure it out, her stomach turning from the up and down movements of the wolves as they now run with her through the forest. She feels like she might throw up at any moment.

But she doesn't. And soon enough she is being carried down into a tunnel and then into the belly of an abandoned shaft from an old mine. The smell of old stale life overwhelms the young woman for a while, and then she suddenly finds herself used to it the deeper they get underground. The wolves stop in one of the many tunnels when they start to hear voices. Then Fia is taken down and unbound. Now they walk her down the tunnels, deeper, toward the voices.

Then the tunnel opens into a cavern. It is an incredible setup, almost temple-like, lit by what looks like hundreds of candles. At the far end, there are twelve men seated on massive thrones that look like they have been carved out of the wall. They look like they are ready to lift off and disappear. They also appear to be glowing. Fia knows exactly what they are. Still, she is not afraid, even with many more vampires in the room looking at her, the ones not attending to the twelve now on her, relieving the wolves of their charge.

She doesn't want to start to believe that the idea of what this all means might just be so. Fia doesn't want to believe it for a second. But why else would she be brought here under such an elaborate guise? What could these vampires want with her that they couldn't get from a million other women? But the truth is that Fia knows in her heart already that her brothers have something to do with this. She can sense that there is a connection between all this and her brothers.

"She is beautiful..." An old vampire seated third from the right speaks so that his voice fills the space.

"Why don't you just kill me? Just kill me! What is this?" Fia needs them to say what her heart needs to be true.

"Beautiful and feisty...she is every bit like her brothers..." The same vampire says the words that Fia needs to hear for her heart to start beating a little faster. She starts to believe that maybe she will get to see her brothers one more time before she dies. Regardless of their strength and bravery, she knows that there is no way that Luke and Tanner can save her or themselves from so much evil.

The vampires chain Fia to one of the walls. It is clear that they are expecting more prisoners from the chains dangling to either side of her. And now she dares hope that her brothers are some of these prisoners. She thinks of this possibility to distract herself as her clothes are removed. At least it is warm where she is thanks to the many candles. The candlelight romanticizes the image of Fia, naked, chained to the wall, and it isn't long before the space starts to hang with a heavy erotic air.

Fia watches the vampires and wolves watching her. She can see that they have arousal hanging between their legs. The vampires move closer and closer to her, some of the wolves too. The twelve vampires on their rock thrones, vampires that Fia has gathered are called The Leadership, just sit comfortably and watch. Her chest starts to heave, and sweat drops form on her breasts as she starts to warm up even more. Now she is anxious, but not about the vampires and wolves. It is the thought that she might see her brothers that has her very anxious indeed.

The vampires seem to have some sort of unspoken carte blanche while they wait. The wolves have once again been sent to get the message to Arianna and Tanner, taking Fia's dress as proof that they have her. Fia's anxiety is now excitement as it becomes clear that she really is going to be seeing Tanner soon. There is no mention of Luke now, not by name, and her heart drops a little. The hands moving up and down her body do nothing to lift her from this.

But her body doesn't have the same attachment to her

family as her heart does, and soon she is becoming very much aroused by the men moving up and down on her with expert precision. They know exactly how to tease her body and make it come to them regardless of the battle of her will. Soon enough the vampires have set Fia on fire and she is moaning as someone touches her between her legs so lightly that she moves her pussy in his direction. The Leadership just watches as her breasts swell and her clit grows into an inviting red plum.

The Leadership warns the vampires to play nicely. Everyone in the room can smell that Fia is still a virgin. The old vampires have decided that once they are done with Tanner and Arianna, they will draw lots for her virginity. They are after all still men, despite their age, with the same virility they've possessed for thousands of years now already; and as much experience. Fia moans some more as her clit is rubbed lightly by many fingers, her breasts sucked by many mouths, and even her lips teased with icy lips that send shivers down her delicate spine.

Her legs are parted as far as the chains on her ankles will allow. She looks down between her legs as a very handsome vampire, who looks no older than she is, gets on his knees in front of her. The others back up a little to give him space to do what he wants to do. They all start rubbing their cocks. The Leadership also starts to shuffle in their seats as their dicks become uncomfortable erections. It isn't too long though before everyone settles into the show and rubs their dick openly, no place for shyness amongst men.

Fia wants to look away. She wants to have no part in engaging with the man between her legs. But it isn't easy; as soon as he places his lips on her clit it is impossible to ignore him. He gives her clit a hard kiss and then a couple of soft ones. Then he kisses her pussy through the softness of her pubic hair. When his lips move up and down on her belly she wants him back on her cunt but won't dare say it, imagining her brothers' disappointment if they should find her enjoying herself with a vampire. The thought of Tanner and Luke gives her the strength to look away from the work being done between her thighs.

However, when he sends his tongue onto her clit she is again looking at him. He really has the most incredible face, sharp features with gentle eyes. Fia can't help but stare. Everyone can see that she is melting toward the man whose tongue is now not only dancing over her pussy but also moving into it, just a little. Fia moves from foot to foot as she tries to stabilize herself. This distracts her licker and so he takes a hand to her thighs and holds her so that her feet stay on the ground.

Fia still manages to shudder despite the firm grip on her thighs. But she isn't going anywhere. And neither is her beautiful punani. She is licked with so many varying degrees of intensity that her mind starts to race wildly. The heat now seems too much as she burns up from the inside. Her pussy sweats from the inside and her juices are licked up enthusiastically. This isn't the disappointment that she had always been told that sex would be. But she isn't having sex. Not yet. Whatever this is though, it's every bit as good as when she touches herself.

After giving her a full and complete orgasm, he makes space for the next vampire with a snaky tongue keen to get into Fia's warmth. Again she is brought to an orgasm, as scintillating as the first one. The vampires wear her out with nothing but their tongues now, and she has forgotten the reality of her situation. Even the hope of seeing her brothers has left her, her body rocking between all the deep heavens she has never even known. But her introduction to these places couldn't be more riddled with contradictions.

Fia doesn't know what to do with her body. Not that she would know what to do with it anyway if the situation was different. Sex in her mind is something that she now imagines to be intense and beautiful. If only she could have had the opportunity to experience it with one of the young men who had always given her lusty looks back in the village. Now her virginity will be lost to an ancient vampire in the bowels of the earth. She has no choice but to accept this now. For a brief moment between orgasms, she remembers her brothers and her mother. But then a tongue is inside her pussy again and the world is a blur...

Tanner is the first to sense that they have company. He helps Arianna dress quickly in borrowed items from shepherds. He too has borrowed what really are pieces of cloth, ripped from cloaks. The pair looks like savages from times gone by. But the warmth of the night makes it acceptable, as long as the important parts of their nakedness are covered.

"Something's here..." Tanner whispers again, putting everyone on edge immediately. Arianna senses it too now and looks around to see where the attack is going to be coming from. There is no fire to protect them, the shepherds needing to save the last bit of oil for the journey home.

Then the wolves step out of the shadows and throw Fia's dress on the ground. Luke goes for the dress and holds it up, recognizing it immediately. He looks at Tanner. "Fia," he says.

Tanner doesn't wait for an explanation. He is on the wolf who held his sister's dress immediately and drives his fangs into the animal's back. He goes straight through the fur and into the rubbery skin. He gets through the veins and injects massive amounts of venom into the wolf while holding it firmly on the ground. Then he lifts the wolf into the air, snaps its neck, and rips it off so violently that everyone has wolf blood on them. The others growl and dive through the air for Tanner.

Luke and the others go toward Tanner, too, to help him. Arianna is quick to stop them. They hold back. She flies into the center of the wolves before they've even reached Tanner and she takes two by the throat. She rips them to shreds and then drops them to the ground. The last wolf growls loudly and then goes in for Tanner. Tanner grabs it and takes a firm hold of its head. He is about to snap its neck when Arianna grabs hold of him.

"Wait Tanner, don't. If you kill him then we won't know how to find your sister..." Arianna speaks loudly and with authority. She looks at Luke for some help.

"Only it knows where Fia is and how to get to her," Luke begs Tanner for their sister's sake.

Tanner lets out a gruesome scream and drops the wolf. Everybody just looks at each other for the longest time. Then the wolf starts to move into the forest slowly, looking back occasionally to see if he is being followed, knowing that he cannot return without Arianna and Tanner. But he knows somehow that they will follow. He knows that there is no way that they will leave their sister to a fate similar to what Arianna had gone through with the vampires.

"You are not coming with us!" Tanner is looking at all of the shepherds but speaking mostly to his brother. "I promise that I'll bring her back. I'll bring her back!"

It takes a lot of convincing but eventually Luke accepts that they will just slow them down. And the sooner they get to Fia, the better. Who knows what is already happening to her. Who knows what must be going through her head. Luke imagines her in some dark place surrounded by animals, beasts that are touching and prodding and taunting her. He can't bring himself to believe that she remembers everything they taught her. He can only see his little sister frightened in the dark by herself.

"Go, brother. And bring her back. But make sure you kill every one of those things. Kill every last one!" Luke and Tanner lock in an embrace and then Arianna and Tanner follow the wolf into the forest. The time has come for them to come face to face with The Leadership.

They move quickly through the night. As they go both Tanner and Arianna know that Fia could already be dead. But they can't go and seen. And even if she is, at least this way they will have found the Leadership. An opportunity like this doesn't come along very often. Arianna is at full strength again. And now she has Tanner, also a vampire, and a powerful one at that. This is a rare opportunity to have all twelve members of The Leadership in the same room and kill them. Or at least try!

"Welcome Arianna...and your friend..." The Leadership seems to speak at the same time, saying the same thing.

Tanner and Arianna don't answer, looking instead at Fia chained to the wall, her pussy still being licked, her breasts still being sucked. There are three vampires working on her, the others now at full attention. The room seems to close in on everyone as the tension of finally having Arianna in their grasp settles over the vampires. She is finally in a vulnerable position and they can bring her reign of inconvenience to an absolute end.

But Tanner isn't as settled into himself as Arianna thought. He is impulsive. And his first impulse is to get to his sister and save her from the beasts threatening her purity. He does just that. One by one he pulls them away from Fia, into the air, rips off their heads, and throws them into the crowd. Then he breaks the chains that are holding his sister up and against the walls and takes her into his arms. Fia lets out a chilling scream as she realizes what her brother is.

"It's me Fia. It's still me." He rocks her in a way that is familiar to her and she remembers the many times he did it when they were children. She rubs her hands over his face and looks deep into his eyes.

"How?" Fia wants to know.

"It doesn't matter. What matters is that you're okay now. I'm going to get you out of here...we're going to get you out of here..." He looks over to Arianna as he finishes his sentence. He puts his sister down and instructs her to stay put.

Arianna looks at the army before them. She looks at the smug leadership grinning at her like she could never be any real sort of threat. Their arrogance is what pisses her off most of all. She looks over at Tanner who isn't moving too far away from his sister, wanting to be close enough to her in case the vampires and wolves got any ideas. There is no need to prolong this with conversation. They are either going to get out alive or they're not, but they're going to put up a hell of a fight trying. And they are definitely not just going to run.

Then Arianna spots it. On a platform in front of the Leadership is a large book. She knows that this must be the fabled book of scrolls that contains the secrets to the vampires' vulnerability. With this, she can go a very long way in saving the world. If she can get this book into the hands of humans like Luke and his friends, then they can become a tiny army of their own. And they can definitely make a significant dent in the vampire population.

Without thinking too much about it, Arianna flies over

the Guard and grabs the first member of The Leadership by the head. She pivots above him rapidly so that she tears off his head while he remains seated. The Guard moves in her direction, too late; she kills three of the Leadership before they are on her. Arianna makes light work of them, killing members of the Guard and members of The Leadership in turn.

Tanner has his hands full too, keeping himself and Fia alive. Arianna keeps screaming for him to get his sister out of here, that she can handle it. But Tanner can't risk not seeing her again. And with The Leadership dead, the Guard will be a walk in the park, especially with two of them fighting. Fia can do nothing but watch. She is happy that more and more vampires are disappearing in incinerated heaps. Tanner and Arianna let none of the wolves escape either.

The battle doesn't last too long even with such a large number of vampires to get through. And soon enough Arianna and Tanner are moving Fia through the tunnels and out into the forest. They fly slowly, shaky after the battle. When they get to Luke and the others they are sitting around a fire, lost in their individual thoughts.

"Luke?!" Fia runs to him just as soon as her feet are on the ground. The others turn their faces so as not to see her nakedness. Luke's shirt covers his sister and then the others greet her properly.

They take in the magnitude of what has just happened, and how all their paths have crossed. Arianna places the book in Luke's hands before explaining to him what it all means. He flips through the pages, the others soon also reading over his shoulders. It isn't long before they realize that they hold the key to their life's mission. And their obsession with and dedication to this mission soon has them rejuvenated and energized.

Arianna and Tanner also have a mission. They have the strength to handle the werewolves and so they are going to go through the world killing every last one of these animals. There isn't a real plan except to find and destroy. It could take a very long time since they don't know how these wolves have placed themselves in the world. There is also no clear understanding of how these animals really developed since no one has ever seen a female werewolf.

The mist settles on the forest floor around them but it isn't cold. Tanner has his arms around Arianna and she settles into his embrace. The moon joins in and bathes them in shimmering white light. The animals in the forest gather closer, feeling the love that is coming from the couple. Tanner and Arianna look like they've belonged to each other forever.

As they kiss, they emit an orange glow that draws even more creatures from the undergrowth. They are the kind of audience that neither of them minds. They just love the fact that the animals don't fear them, despite what they are. It makes them feel almost human. With their tongues dancing around in each other's mouths, they light up the forest beautifully.

As they make love they turn up the soft earth and toss the leaves around. The audience becomes ever more embarrassed as the passion takes more and more of an intense turn and they make their way to their night hideouts, leaving Tanner and Arianna to just enjoy the night. It isn't going to be their last night like this, but there is going to be a lot of hard work ahead. They are going to have to hunt the wolves down until they are sure that they have killed every last one.

They will also help the seven with the vampires every chance they get.

For now, though, it's all about the two of them. Tanner moves deep into Arianna and she lifts up off the earth against each of his downward thrusts. He lets her lift them a little and then gently pushes her back into the ground with a long stroke. He doesn't make a single mistake with each stroke, driving into her with love and passion, pleasing every part of her with just one solid part of him. Arianna hasn't felt safe and vulnerable all at once in almost eight hundred years.

They make love through the night, almost daring the impending dawn to try and disrupt them. But it's not necessary to tempt fate. They've had enough near-fatal run-ins with her already. Tanner is the one lifting them off the ground now. He flies Arianna to safety with himself still inside her. There is no way that he is going to separate from his love now, wrapped in the deliciousness of their union.

In the safety of their cove, the couple continues loving each other. The sun bathes the world in orange while Tanner and Arianna turn their love nest into their own kind of orange. The heat moves between them and around them so that the sweat is dripping down every part of them. There is nothing that can disturb them now, and they lock into each other in the heat of the day before resting up for their nighttime activity. As soon as the sun sets completely, Arianna and Tanner will start their mission to make the world a safer place...

ABOUT THE AUTHOR

Shala Breece is an emerging erotica author of many erotica kinks and sub-genres. Be sure to check out other books and leave a review if this story got you hot!

Visit my blog at Shala Breece Blog

Join my newsletter for exclusive Shala Breece Newsletter

Sign up for Free Stories from Xplicit Press Authors

Xplicit Press Author Updates

Like Xplicit Press on Facebook

Follow Xplicit Press on Twitter

Readers: I want to expand a few of the stories to see where the characters can be explored further. If there are any of the stories that you would like to read more about again, I'd love to hear from you!

Keep In Touch
Shala Breece
info@shalabreece.com

www.ingramcontent.com/pod-product-compliance
Lightning Source LLC
Chambersburg PA
CBHW021151130626
46554CB00005B/1758